# Edwin of
# the
# Iron
# Shoes

# Edwin of the Iron Shoes

*a novel of suspense by*
*Marcia Muller*

David McKay Company, Inc.
Ives Washburn, Inc.
New York

Library of Congress Cataloging in Publication Data

Muller, Marcia.
  Edwin of the iron shoes.

  (MW suspense)
  I. Title.
PZ4.M9594Ed      [PS3563.U397]      813'.5'4      77-8564
ISBN 0-679-50782-5

                    10 9 8 7 6 5 4 3 2 1

        MANUFACTURED IN THE UNITED STATES OF AMERICA

*To Fred Gilson*
*and my family*

Edwin of
the
Iron
Shoes

# One

I stood next to the car, waiting for the number ninety-three trolley to pass, its antennae zinging along the overhead cable. The lighted windows of the trolley were empty except for the driver and a lone passenger. It was two thirty in the morning.

When the street was clear, I crossed to where the flashing lights of the cop cars and the ambulance were reflected against the black, wet pavement. The situation must be pretty bad, all right.

I'd been jerked from my sleep about forty-five minutes earlier by the insistent ring of the telephone and my employer's voice saying, "Sharon, get yourself up and meet me over at Salem Street, Joan Albritton's shop."

Hank Zahn, senior associate at All Souls Cooperative, the San Francisco legal services plan, knew better than to call his staff investigator in the middle of the night without a good reason. I pulled myself up on one elbow and said, "Don't tell me someone's set another fire over there?"

"Worse. A lot worse. This time it's murder."

"Give me half an hour to get there." In the middle of

saying it, I realized he'd hung up without telling me who had been killed.

Now, as I pushed my way through the crowd of onlookers, I spotted Hank in the doorway of Joan Albritton's antique shop, talking with a big blond-haired man in a tan trench coat. Hank was almost as tall as the other man, but next to him he looked gawky, as if his long limbs were fastened together at the joints with paper clips. As usual, he had come out in the rain without a coat, and his corduroy jacket was dark with water stains. The dampness had made his light-brown hair curl even more tightly than normal.

When I approached, Hank held out an arm and drew me under the protection of the doorway. "This is Ms. McCone, Sharon McCone, my staff investigator," he said to the big man. To me he added, "Lieutenant Gregory Marcus, Homicide."

Marcus's eyes flickered sharply over me from under bushy eyebrows several shades darker than his hair. "You're the young woman who's been investigating the arsons and vandalisms down here?" He made a gesture that took in the whole block.

I said I was.

Marcus hesitated, the corner of his mouth twitching, and I braced myself for one of the variants of the usual remark, along the lines of "what's-a-nice-girl-like-you-doing-mixed-up-with-an-ugly-business-like-this?"

But the lieutenant spared me that. Instead, his mouth turned down and he said, "We'll want a statement from you, but tomorrow'll be time enough. There's nothing we can do now but let the lab boys finish and get the body out of here."

He turned away abruptly and motioned to a uniformed officer.

I clutched Hank's arm with cold fingers. "Who, Hank? You didn't tell me who."

"Joan Albritton."

I could feel Hank's expression of dismay mirrored on my own face. Joan Albritton, his client, was an energetic,

2

cheerful little antique dealer who, at fifty-seven, had more vitality than most people half her age. Was? Had been.

"Oh, my God," I said softly. "Who did it?"

"They don't know. There aren't any leads. They think she was stabbed with one of her own knives, from a case of valuable pieces next to the cash register."

I began to shudder and barely managed to control it. When I could talk, I asked, "How'd you find out so fast?"

"Charlie Cornish called me." Charlie was the owner of Junk Emporium, across the street. "We might as well go over to his place. He's got some coffee on, and there's nothing we can do here."

I released his arm. "No, you go ahead. I'll be over in a few minutes."

They were bringing the body out now, and in our retreat from the doorway to the sidewalk, I lost Hank in the crowd. The rain had turned into a fine mist—typical San Francisco weather for February. I looked once at the covered form strapped to the stretcher, then looked away and as I did, I spotted Lt. Marcus.

I pushed through the bystanders toward him and caught his attention.

"Lieutenant Marcus, do you think I could take a look around the shop?"

He hesitated, regarding me. "Zahn's investigator, huh?" Then he shrugged and ushered me through the doorway.

Three concrete steps led down into the shop, which was set a few feet below street level. I stumbled going down and felt Marcus's hand at my elbow, steadying me. The front room, usually dim and cavernous, was illuminated by floodlights.

My attention went immediately to the chalk outline on the floor near the ancient cash register. It was not a very big outline: Joan Albritton had been a tiny woman. She had fallen on her side, one arm askew. I tried to ignore the dark stains on the faded Oriental carpet.

Automatically I glanced at the little barred windows,

3

which in daytime admitted feeble rays of light to the shop.

"No, it wasn't a break-in," Marcus said impatiently. "There's no sign of forced entry, either here or in the workroom behind. Whoever it was, she let him in."

His hand still rested on my elbow. I moved away from him.

"The knife was from this case?" I indicated a small glass cabinet where Joan Albritton had kept her most valuable small items: jewelry, silverware, old coins.

He nodded. "Presumably. You'll notice a set of bone-handled knives—they're more like daggers, actually. One is missing. The medical examiner says Albritton's wounds could have been caused by it."

I examined the case, not touching it even though the powder dustings told me the fingerprint man had finished. Four double-edged knives with roughly cut bone handles nestled in a velvet-lined case. A space for a fifth knife was empty. The blades were long and wicked-looking. I swallowed hard.

I said, "She always kept this locked, with the key on a little chain around her neck."

"Not tonight. The key's in the lock." Marcus pointed at the slender gold chain hanging from it. The chain was intact.

"Then she must have opened it herself. Who found her?"

"Fellow across the street. A man named Cornish. He says he knew she was here late taking inventory—end of February, you know—and thought she might need a cup of coffee. The door was open, and he found her." Marcus gestured at the chalk marks.

I sighed and turned around, taking in the rest of the shop, unfamiliar in the glare of light. The big room was packed wall to wall with furniture: sofas, tables, bureaus, chairs. Little aisles large enough for only one person meandered haphazardly throughout. On tabletops and chair seats stood the smaller wares: vases, pictures, lamps, old books.

I moved down the aisles, feeling Marcus's eyes on me as I mechanically touched some of Joan's beloved objects: Clothilde, a French dressmaker's dummy; Bruno, the stuffed

4

German shepherd; Edwin of the Iron Shoes. These were special, not for sale, inanimate friends to whom Joan Albritton had talked as she went about her busy days at the shop.

I stopped in front of Edwin, the little boy mannequin whose feet had been fitted with an ornate pair of iron shoes. Edwin, Joan had told me, was an art lover. He stood, staring at an oil painting of a Madonna and child on the wall beside him.

I turned and saw Marcus. He was looking at me with a frown. In my business, I often annoyed people, but I couldn't think of anything I'd done that might have provoked the lieutenant.

I ignored his look and said, "Thanks for letting me see the shop."

He nodded. "I want you to come down first thing tomorrow morning and give us the background on this street. Arson cases, weren't they?"

"Arson, and other types of vandalism: brick throwing, littering, smoke bombs. There were several bad fires, which is why the two buildings on either side of this are empty. I was asked to come in because the merchants thought someone wanted to buy the land as a parcel and was trying to force them out. And that is precisely what happened: the city condemned all the buildings in this and the next block less than two weeks after I came on the case."

"Why you?"

"Why was I the one to investigate? Hank Zahn is—was—Joan Albritton's attorney. When the merchants didn't get much help from the police, she called Hank for advice, and he sent me out to talk to her. I often do jobs like that for All Souls' clients."

When I'd said that about help from the police, Marcus's lips had tightened, but he only said, "Interesting. Don't forget about that statement, will you?"

I said I wouldn't and preceded him out of the shop. The ambulance had pulled away and the crowd was dispersing. Across the street, a light burned in the front windows of Junk Emporium. Hank was probably waiting for me, drinking

5

coffee with Charlie Cornish, so I started over. I wanted to talk to Charlie, hoping that despite his grief, he might remember something useful to add to my statement for the police.

# Two

I tapped on the door of Junk Emporium. A moment later a tall, gray-haired man of about fifty-five, clad in old army fatigues, opened it. Charlie Cornish's tiny eyes were rimmed with red, and his long mane was tangled, as if he'd been clawing at it with his fingers.

"I'm sorry, Charlie. She meant a lot to you."

"Yeah. Yeah. Come on in. There's coffee on the hot plate. I was going to ask Joanie if she wanted to come over for some when . . ." His voice grated harshly and broke.

I stepped into the shop. A dim bulb in a green glass shade lit the corner Charlie used as an office. A two-burner hot plate stood on the scarred oak desk, and Hank sat on a straight chair beside it. When he saw me, he got up and filled a cracked china cup with coffee. He handed it to me, then glanced anxiously at Charlie, who had slumped down into his old swivel chair.

The thing I liked most about Hank, a good friend as well as employer, was his concern for other people. One of its offshoots was All Souls, a cooperative he and three other

7

attorneys had founded to provide quality legal service at reasonable prices to its member clients. Hank was thirty-five and had practiced family law for nine years, but he'd never gotten cynical nor lost his empathy for his fellow humans. Now he shifted his troubled eyes from Charlie to me and back again.

I sat down beside him on another straight chair and shivered. Around us the junk—old stoves, mattresses, crude wooden furniture—hulked in the darkness.

I asked Charlie as gently as I could, "What time did you find her?"

"About one thirty." Charlie rubbed his red eyes. "I was worried about her, working so late all alone over there. I knew she hadn't had supper, and I thought a break would do her good. The door was open when I got there, and Joanie . . ." His voice trailed off, and he rested his head in his hands.

I looked at Hank, then took a big sip of coffee.

"You're going to find out who did it." Charlie's words were a flat statement.

"I think that's a job for the police," I said. "They're certainly more capable than I am."

"The police!" Charlie spat it out. "What did they do for us last fall, when we were getting our windows smashed and our buildings torched off? Bunch of crummy buildings, small-time shopkeepers: the cops couldn't be bothered. The hell with the police!"

"But, Charlie, a murder . . . " I'd been involved in murder investigations before, but generally my work was more routine. All Souls' clients were a nonviolent bunch: solid citizens, often minority group members, with lower to middle incomes. A typical client entertained liberal sentiments, toyed with the idea of an "alternative" lifestyle, and would never get busted for anything more serious than growing marijuana plants on the fire escape.

"Look, Sharon," Charlie insisted, "the merchants here need somebody who's going to think of their interests,

8

Joanie's interests. The cops don't give a damn about us!"

I looked at Hank again. "It depends on what Hank says, Charlie. I'm the only investigator at All Souls. The other attorneys there need me to collect evidence for suits, interview witnesses. . . . I can't drop everything."

Charlie turned to Hank. "Well, are you going to let her work on Joanie's murder or aren't you?"

Hank shrugged and scratched at his curly head, his typical gesture of agitation. "Joan Albritton was a client, same as any other member of the cooperative. I guess you could say our obligation extends beyond her death." He hesitated a moment, and then a mischievous gleam came into his eyes. "Why not? Go ahead and investigate. Before you joined our staff, we were used to doing our own research. This may be just what my lazy colleagues need to get them in shape again."

I felt a stirring of excitement. Murder cases didn't come along every day, and I did feel a personal commitment to this one. Even though I hadn't known Joan Albritton very long, she was the sort of person who quickly made her way into your affections and brightened your world with her mere presence. Her death hurt me, much more than I was willing to show in front of Charlie. His own grief was burden enough without me adding mine to it.

"Okay," I said, "if you want me to, I'll see what I can find out."

"You didn't find out who was doing all that before."

The suddenness of Charlie's change of attitude surprised me, but his accusation didn't sting. It was a fact. I hadn't found out anything of value. "That's right. But the disturbances stopped, didn't they?"

"Until this."

I nodded. That, too, I could not deny.

Hank cleared his throat. "You have to be fair, Charlie. Sharon had it narrowed down, but she couldn't get the proof. Without proof . . . "

"The hell with your proof! What good is your proof doing Joanie tonight?" Charlie ran his fingers through his tangled gray hair. "I go over there, the door's partway open, and she's lying there, so still. I call her, feel for her pulse. Nothing. Blood on the carpet. On Joanie's Oriental carpet! And you talk about proof!"

I asked, "The glass case was open?"

"Yes. It had been open since . . . since she started taking the inventory, I guess. She would have to inventory each piece of jewelry and the other little stuff, wouldn't she?"

"I guess so. Did you notice one of the knives was missing then?"

"That's right. They're awful knives, so sharp. . . . " His voice faltered and stopped.

"Did you see anything else unusual? Anything else that was out of place or missing?"

"Unusual?" His grief exploded in my face. "With Joanie lying there dead? Wasn't that unusual enough? If you'd stopped the vandals when things first started getting out of hand, she'd be alive right now!"

I realized how stupid my question must have sounded to him and immediately wished I'd been more tactful.

"Charlie," Hank said gently, "you know it isn't Sharon's fault."

"No, Hank, no. He's probably right." I steered the conversation back onto the track. "But we can waste all the time we want in recriminations, and it won't get us any closer to the killer. Do you want me to find him or don't you, Charlie?"

The hard words calmed him. "I guess, as president of the Merchants' Association, I'm empowered to hire you. We'll have to have a formal vote on it, of course, but the others'll go along with whatever I say." With a wry grin he added, "It's a tradition of the Association to go along with the president. Otherwise, the members might have to do some work."

It struck me then, as it always did when I spent time with Charlie, that he didn't talk like a junk dealer. I wondered about him: his background, his education, where he'd come

10

from. But I wasn't going to get any answers, not from Charlie Cornish; he liked to perpetuate the myth that he had sprung full-blown from the pavement of Salem Street twenty years before. Maybe Joan Albritton, his closest friend and sometime lover, had known, but his secret was now lost with her.

To Hank I said, "What about this Lieutenant . . . Marcus, is it?"

"What about him?"

"If he's in charge of the case, how's he going to feel about a private operator snooping around his territory?"

"Greg Marcus is one of the more cooperative detectives on the force. I saw him letting you in to look at the shop, after all. I think I can work out a deal with him, maybe something to do with the estate, which I'll be handling. It's possible you could finish the end-of-year inventory; we'll need an evaluation for estate purposes. That would give you access to the place, and you could figure out if anything's missing."

I hesitated.

"Now what's wrong?" Hank asked.

"This Lieutenant Marcus, I don't think he'll go along with that. He let me in, but he doesn't seem to like me."

Hank snorted. "He doesn't know you. Greg's a bachelor and old-fashioned. He probably wonders what a pretty little girl like you is doing out this late at night."

I smiled. "Well, okay, if you say so and can work something out."

"I'm sure I can."

I hoped he was right. I wanted, very badly, to find out who had killed the chubby little antique dealer.

Charlie broke into the conversation. "Then it's settled. I'll meet with the other merchants as soon as I can get them together."

I had a sudden thought. "Has anyone notified Joan's family?"

Charlie looked bleak. "What family? After her grandson died last summer, I was all she had left. And I'm not much."

11

"I'd forgotten." Come to think of it, there might be a lot I'd forgotten since the previous fall. In October, Hank had sent me down to Salem Street, San Francisco's mecca for collectors of both the valuable and the cheap, to talk with Joan Albritton about the fires and vandalisms plaguing the owners of seventeen antique and junk shops located there. The fires, Joan was sure, had been set in an effort to force the merchants out of their run-down buildings, which stood on desirable land near the Civic Center.

Now I said to Charlie, "Joan told me there were four principal owners of the property in these two blocks, all merchants. Right? There's you and her, Austin Bigby and Dan Efron."

"Right. Joanie and I have the largest holdings, then Austin. Dan has the smallest. When the city condemned our buildings last fall, we decided to sell as a parcel. That's the way we could get the best price. And since Joanie had the best head for business, we figured whatever she recommended would be okay for the rest of us, providing no one had any serious objections. However you looked at it, we'd get our equity out, plus some."

"So the Association accepted bids and was planning to announce a decision by March first?"

"That's right. We had to be out by May one, so that left plenty of time for the formalities."

"Had Joan decided which bid to accept?" Hank asked. "The deadline was getting close."

"She was having a hard time. I figured it was because she had a lot on her mind, like trying to find new space for her shop. But then, this last week, something came over her." Charlie shook his head and took a long swig of coffee. "I can't imagine Joanie without her shop, but I got the impression she was thinking of retiring."

"Did she actually mention retirement to you?" I asked.

"No, she didn't mention it," he said shortly. "I've got the feeling there were a lot of things she wasn't telling me lately."

"Like what?"

Charlie smiled faintly. "Well, if she wasn't discussing them with me, I wouldn't know, would I?"

I sighed and then turned briskly to Hank. "I think it's time we got going. Tomorrow's likely to be a long day, and there's not much sleeping time left."

He got to his feet. "Can you drop me at All Souls? I had to take a cab down here."

"Sure."

Charlie followed us to the door. "I'll be in touch as soon as the Association meets."

We stepped out into the street. The rain had stopped, and a wind, warm for February, was blowing. Behind us, I heard Charlie turn the double locks on the flimsy door.

"He's really broken up," Hank said as we started down the street.

"He ought to be. Joan Albritton was the one good thing in his life."

"I guess so. It's not much of a life, living in one room behind that shop full of trash, cooking off a hot plate. How can he stand it?"

"Maybe he likes trash. You might say he's made it his life."

We got to my car, Hank carefully folding his six-foot frame into the passenger seat of the battered red MG. "You're really going home to sleep?"

"Of course not. I'm going to All Souls with you. I want to read over my files on those vandalisms."

"Think you'll find anything there?"

"I don't know, but it's the only starting place I've got, so I'd better check it out."

# Three

Eight forty-five in the morning. I stretched my arms above my head and yawned, pushing the swivel chair away from the old office desk. My scribbled notes on the Salem Street vandalisms littered its surface. They had been a place to start, but that was all. Certainly they hadn't told me anything I didn't already know.

On the surface, any of the bidders for the condemned buildings might have begun the campaign of harassment, hoping to force the merchants out. After dozens of interviews, though, I'd ruled out three of the four contenders.

First, Hemphill College of Law, which wanted the land for an expanded campus. Talks with various officials had convinced me that violence wasn't their style. They might take advantage of political pull, since the college trustees had high standing in the community. But violence? Never.

The real-estate syndicate headed by a Mrs. Cara Ingalls I ruled out for similar reasons. I hadn't been able to meet with Mrs. Ingalls herself, but from several of her associates I judged the syndicate had too much financial weight to stoop to petty crime. If their plans to build a complex of shops and condominiums near the Civic Center were that important, they would merely raise their offer until it became irresistible to the merchants. That the property might not be available at any price would never enter their minds.

The New Freedom School, a sort of kindergarten for adults, hoped to buy the parcel for their new facilities. The teachers and administrators treated me to a great deal of rhetoric about getting in touch with my feelings and expressing myself, but they meant emotional and sexual self-expression rather than the violent physical variety. I couldn't imagine any of them having either the organization or the initiative to carry through a plan of intimidation.

The Western Addition Credit Union: now there was the group I suspected. Skilled in federal grantmanship, they had started as a shoestring operation and parlayed themselves into a position of wide influence in the black community. WACU grabbed up government funding as soon as it became available, administering an incredible number of programs, from food-stamp distribution to minority business development, and now they hoped to construct a state-funded low-income housing project on Salem Street.

I'd talked with the credit union leaders long enough to realize they were people who would let nothing stand in the way of their objectives, and when I found some of their pamphlets in a mountain of trash littering Charlie Cornish's sidewalk, I felt I was on the right track. This, however, was not the concrete proof I needed, and it might just have been evidence of someone else's cleverness.

Then, abruptly, the vandalism had stopped, the day before the merchants received notice from the city that the buildings would be condemned. And hours after the notice, it was the WACU that made the first bid for the properties. Still, it could have been a chain of coincidences. It certainly was no basis for bringing charges of arson and vandalism against them.

After the buildings had been condemned, my involvement

with the Salem Street merchants had ended. Ended, that is, until last night, when some unknown person had gone far beyond mere destruction of property.

I stuffed my notes back into the file and locked it in my desk drawer. At least my memory was refreshed for the meeting with Lt. Marcus. I realized I was worried about making a good impression on the man, and I felt a flash of annoyance with myself.

Look, I thought, you're not normally an anxious-to-please type, so stop fussing over this statement.

I put the surly lieutenant out of my mind and left my office. Following the smell of coffee and frying bacon, I went down the long hallway to the kitchen at the back of the house. These were not smells you'd find around your average law firm, but All Souls was in no way average.

The cooperative was housed in a big brown Victorian in the Bernal Heights District of San Francisco. On the first floor, in addition to the kitchen and living room, were the offices, and several of the attorneys, including Hank Zahn, lived on the second. A legal services plan that adjusted its fees to its clients' incomes did not pay princely salaries, so the free room and kitchen privileges were a welcome subsidy. I, for one, doubted I'd last in such a communal situation for more than two days, but I had to admit All Souls was a nice place to hang around, especially at mealtimes.

This morning, though, I wasn't hungry, and the excited chatter about "our murder" got on my nerves. I left a note for Hank, still asleep upstairs, and drove the few blocks to my studio apartment on Guerrero Street, in the Mission District.

I needed to change, since the soft red jumpsuit, the nearest thing at hand when I'd dressed earlier that morning, didn't seem decorous enough for police headquarters. While my coffee perked, I took a quick shower, then drank a cup as I dressed in a tailored denim pantsuit. I pulled my long black hair back in a tortoise-shell barrette and wondered, as I did several times a week, if I should get it cut. In spite of my almost thirty years and the gray streak that had been there since my teens, the hair still made me look very much the ingenue. Then, annoyed at the conservative notions I was developing, I yanked the barrette out, brushed vigorously, and went off to the SFPD with my hair blowing free in the breeze.

Might as well be yourself, Sharon, I thought.

Sneakily, a little voice added, Greg Marcus isn't going to like you no matter what you do.

# *Four*

Lt. Marcus leaned back in his chair and waited until the stenographer closed the door as she left the cubicle. He then shifted his blue eyes to me, neutral eyes, neither cold nor friendly. His facial expression was a careful blank.

We had been on our best behavior as I gave my statement: he listening attentively while I spoke, leaving out none of the details, including my suspicions of the Western Addition Credit Union. I wondered if now was the time for our fragile rapport to fall apart.

He cleared his throat and began, "I had a call from Hank Zahn earlier."

I nodded and waited for him to go on.

He seemed to pick his next words carefully. "You've got to realize that Zahn and the others at All Souls have been very cooperative with the department in the past. Otherwise, I wouldn't even consider Hank's suggestion, in spite of his being a good personal friend."

Marcus's mention of a friendship with Hank surprised me. On the surface, no two men were more different. Hank had a boyish, accommodating manner that masked his intelligence and stubborn determination. Marcus, on the other hand, projected a rough, no-nonsense image. Hank, in spite of his experience, was still an idealist. Marcus looked as if he had no ideals left.

He went on, "Hank wants me to allow you access to the Salem Street shop, since he needs the completed inventory for the estate. Now, we all know what he really wants you to do. You'll be able to come and go freely down there, and considering your familiarity with the neighborhood, you may be able to pick up a few things that we wouldn't." He paused to light a cigarette, flicking the match at the ashtray with an irritated motion.

"We are," he said, "to be informed of whatever you find out. Immediately. And completely. Do you understand?"

"You've made it clear."

Greg Marcus was not a man I cared to tangle with. Everything about him was tough and disciplined: the controlled quality of his speech; his tight, economical movements; the lean, trim body—a damned good body for a man who must be in his early forties. This morning, probably after no more sleep than I'd gotten, Marcus was clear-eyed and immaculately dressed in a conservative blue suit. His only concession to cheerfulness was a wide tie in a red poppy design. I wondered who had picked the tie for him.

"Just so long as it's clear to you." His eyes settled on my face once more, the brows creased in a frown. I thought I saw the ghost of a perplexed expression there, but for no more than an instant.

He asked, "Do you really have an investigator's license?"

"Yes, I do. Would you like to see it?" I reached for my bag.

He waved a hand at me. "Forget it. I'll take your word. How'd you get into the business?"

"I was in security. Department store security. After a couple of years, I couldn't see spending my life snooping

20

through racks of dresses with a walkie-talkie in my purse. So I went to college and studied sociology."

"Ah, yes. I remember my own soc major. And now, because of your studies, you know all there is to know about criminals, right?" He raised an eyebrow mockingly.

"Very little. When I got out of school, I couldn't get a job. Nobody wants a college graduate with a lot of vague textbook knowledge. So I went to work in security again, for one of the big outfits here in the city, and eventually they trained me for detective work. But in their kind of business, you don't see many criminals. What you see are mostly straying husbands and wives."

He smiled, a hard smile. "Yeah, a nice business. So now you're out on your own, on the way to becoming a super-sleuth."

He was pushing too hard. I kept my voice level. "I'm not on my own; I'm an employee of All Souls. I joined them after the detective agency fired me for refusing to jump at a special assignment that would have humiliated me and set up an innocent man for a very messy and expensive divorce. And I don't know about being what you call a 'super-sleuth.' I'm competent. I'd say my strong point is knowing how to ask the right questions. Without trying to cram my words into other people's mouths."

He sat up straighter and blinked. "Jesus, what next?" he asked softly.

"I'm sorry?"

"Never mind. You wouldn't understand. To get back to the subject, I spoke to that Cornish fellow this morning, and he has an extra set of keys to Albritton's shop. The contents of the shop are yours to inventory. I hope you know something about antiques."

"I don't, but I'll learn."

"I have no doubt you will." He lit another cigarette and leaned back. "What do you think of Cornish anyway?" He asked it casually, but there had to be more than a casual

21

interest behind his question.

Cautiously I said, "Charlie is not an easy person to know. He's a man without a past, except for the twenty years he's spent on Salem Street. Joan Albritton was close to him, but how close I don't know."

Marcus nodded and waited for me to go on.

"I think the relationship had cooled off recently. Joan lost her grandson last summer—he was eighteen and had lived with her most of his life. Charlie told me he felt Joan hadn't discussed a lot of things with him since."

"They were lovers, Charlie and Joan?"

"I think they had been. They still spent a lot of time together, running back and forth between the two shops, cooking meals on Charlie's hot plate. I guess Charlie dropped around at Joan's apartment on Potrero Hill, too. Joan was an amazing woman: cheerful, imaginative, a bundle of energy. Charlie said her grandson's death had slowed her down, but I can't imagine how she could have been more . . . vital."

"How did the grandson die?"

"Of a drug overdose. I understand he had musical talent and had been accepted at Juilliard for the fall. He and Joan were saving the money so he could go, and he had a part-time job with a rock group. That's where the drug trouble came in: he'd already been picked up once for possession and was waiting trial on that charge. It—his death—was a terrible blow to Joan—she'd been sort of reliving her dreams through him."

"How so?"

"Joan had wanted to be an artist. I think she had a fine arts degree from Cal. But she made a bad marriage and ended up an antique dealer. The grandson was like her second chance."

"What about the kid's parents?"

"Died when he was a baby. I don't know the details. He was Joan's last living relative. Charlie's about the closest

22

thing to family she had left, and I guess Joan was all he had, too."

Marcus looked thoughtful. "You picked all that up from asking the right questions? Without cramming words in their mouths, of course."

I shrugged. "I look like someone people can confide in, I guess."

"Do you now?" Marcus paused, studying my face. "You're part Indian, aren't you?"

I nodded. "I'm what they call a 'throwback.' I've only got about an eighth Shoshone blood, but for some reason it all came out in me."

"Interesting," he said. "It didn't come out in anyone else in your family?"

"No. My brothers and sisters are all fair and look like the Scotch-Irish brats they are."

Marcus sat there in silence, his eyes still on my face. I wanted to glance away, but I held my ground. Was he seeing me? Or was he seeing someone else, someone labeled for a private reason of his own as "adversary"?

Marcus broke eye contact first and stood up, indicating dismissal. I stood up, too.

"I'll have the preliminary report from the medical examiner later today, if you're interested," he said. "You'll be in touch?"

"Of course."

"Good luck learning all about antiques." He held out his hand.

I clasped it briefly. "Thank you. I have the feeling it will be quite a job." And an unwelcome one at that, I thought ruefully, since I had no interest at all in antiques, except as a possible motive for murder.

23

# *Five*

As I arrived at Salem Street, a sleek white Mercedes pulled up to the curb in front of Junk Emporium. A short, powerfully built man in a gray three-piece suit got out. He turned and, seeing me on the sidewalk, raised a hand in greeting.

"Hello! You're Sharon McCone, aren't you?"

I recognized Oliver van Osten, a salesman from whom Joan had bought many of her antiques. "Yes, I am. How are you?"

"Shocked, really. This murder is a terrible thing." He crossed to where I stood, giving me plenty of time to appreciate his Prussian good looks and the crisp way he handled himself. I'd met van Osten on two previous occasions at Joan's shop but had never gotten past a nodding acquaintance with him.

He took my hand and grinned, showing even teeth in a wide smile. "Nice to see you again. What are you doing in the neighborhood? Has there been more vandalism?"

"No. I'm here about the murder."

The smile faded, and he dropped my hand. "You're investigating it?"

"That, and taking the final inventory of the goods in the shop. I work for Joan Albritton's attorney."

"Of course." He frowned. "But what do you know of antiques?"

"Not a thing. Maybe you could give me some pointers."

Van Osten's smile returned. "I'll be glad to." He glanced at his watch. "I have a full schedule of calls today, but tomorrow morning I'm free."

"Fine. I'll be at the shop then."

He looked delighted. "I always wanted to be part of a whodunnit. You and I will make a good team of sleuths!"

His gaiety struck a discordant note in light of Joan's death. Hoping to get rid of him I said, "I have to get the key from Charlie now."

"I was on my way to see him, too." Van Osten slipped an arm around my shoulders. "Let's go together."

I had never been a demonstrative person, and people who behaved so freely with comparative strangers startled me. Watch out, Sharon, I warned myself. Remember, this one's a not-too-subtle charmer.

When I had met van Osten the previous October, I realized within minutes why he had the reputation of being a good salesman. He greeted me warmly, wrapped me in an easy flow of conversation, and quickly let me know he thought me a very special person. Only later, when I was away from his dominating presence, did I realize how carefully calculated his whole act was. That, to me, made him someone to be wary of.

This morning, as van Osten and I approached, Charlie sat tipped back in a straight chair in the doorway of Junk Emporium.

The big junkman looked better today than he had the night before. His tiny eyes were still red, but he'd combed his long gray mane and put on a fresh set of olive drab fatigues. I'd never seen Charlie in anything else.

When he saw us, he got up and said, "You're here for Joanie's keys. I'll get my set." He went into his shop and returned a few seconds later with two keys on a chain

26

attached to a puffy ball of bright-pink fur. I stared at it, nestled in his outstretched hand.

Charlie smiled sheepishly. "It's a security puff. Joanie gave it to me. When you're depressed, you're supposed to hold it and sort of meditate. The nice feel of it cheers you up."

I asked, "Does it work?"

He shrugged. "Sometimes. Not today. I tried it, but it didn't work today."

Van Osten cleared his throat and said, "Charlie, I'm sorry about Joan's death."

Charlie turned to him. "Aw, Ollie, we all are."

The salesman winced at the nickname. "It must have been an awful shock to you." He began asking questions, the same questions I'd asked Charlie the night before: when had he found the body, were there any leads. I listened, thinking he might turn up something I didn't know.

As I did, I watched van Osten, disregarding his carefully constructed facial expressions and looking straight into his eyes. Instinctively I stepped away from him, closer to Charlie. I was recoiling from what I had seen, for despite his sympathetic words to Charlie, his eyes were totally devoid of emotion.

Both men suddenly glanced at me, each with an undefinable ability to make me nervous. Charlie, too, seemed menacing. In my confusion, I muttered something about getting started on the inventory and fled across the street to Joan's shop.

The warm air inside the shop smelled stale. A few pale rays of sunlight filtered through the bars on the little windows. Except for the chalk marks and stains on the floor, it was much as I remembered it. Except for that, and the absence of Joan's cheery greeting.

I took off my jacket and draped it over a chair near the cash register, then sat down on the mauve velvet settee next to Clothilde. Forcing my mind away from van Osten's awful eyes, I queried the headless dummy, "Now, where the hell am I supposed to begin?"

I had a lot to learn. Didn't antique dealers refer to

furniture by periods, for instance? Chippendale, Hepple-white, Louis XIV? How was I ever going to be able to attach a meaningful label to each and every object in the shop, plus keep my eyes open for clues to the killer?

I smiled faintly, picturing my finished inventory: "One old table, three older chairs, one whatchamacallit, four some-thing-or-others, one object that looks like it could be an umbrella stand." A crash course in antiques was in order; I'd have to stop by the library later on to pick up some general books on the subject.

Joan had been an expert. She'd been a dealer for twenty years or more and could tell the value and antecedents of any piece after a single glance. When a customer came in, she had a way of drawing him or her into a fantasy world, where every object in the shop came alive with its own special past. I felt a fresh sensation of loss as I remembered the first time I'd come to the shop, early last October.

A tiny, gray-haired woman in a blue smock and slacks had greeted me, a feather duster in her hand. "Welcome to Joan's Unique Antiques!" she'd announced with a wide grin. "I'm Joan Albritton, and this is Clothilde."

She gestured at the headless figure on the settee. The dummy was clad in a long gown of red sequins, which clashed horribly with the mauve upholstery.

"Clothilde," Joan Albritton had gone on, with a glance at me, "used to be an extremely successful *haute couture* model in Paris, and still would be had it not been for her foolish heart. You see, she fell in love with a man from San Francisco and followed him here, only to find he was married, with thirteen kids. So she ended up on Salem Street working for me and pining for her lost love. You can tell she completely lost her head over the fellow!"

I chuckled and bowed to Clothilde. "Pleased to meet you."

Joan's sharp eyes watched me with pleasure. "Maybe you prefer children to glamour girls though. Come this way." She led me down an aisle, stopping here and there to flick the feather duster at imaginary cobwebs.

"This is Edwin of the Iron Shoes, named for his very uncomfortable footgear."

The mannequin, aloof, stared away from us, his pale-blue eyes fixed on the wall. His face had a semi-gloss to it, and the artist who had painted his features onto the carved wood had given him apple cheeks, blossoming with health.

"Hello, Edwin," I said.

Joan's smile grew wider. "Personally, I think Edwin would have preferred a pair of tennis shoes, don't you? As it is, he's been forced into a life of contemplating the arts instead of running around with the other little boys. Edwin's not for sale, but the painting is. I have to change it often so he doesn't get bored."

With his halo of painted gold hair and little boy's sailor suit, Edwin looked very much the innocent on a first trip to the art museum. The painting he studied was of some shepherds and their flock, in a wheat-colored field. The landscape reminded me of parts of Italy or, for that matter, parts of Southern California. The shepherds didn't look too different from some of the fellows I saw walking around San Francisco.

"Are you an art lover by any chance?" Joan Albritton asked me.

"I don't know much about art, probably less than Edwin does. It's a nice painting, though."

"Oh. Oh, yes, it is." She turned from Edwin and led me toward the front of the shop.

"Of course, there's Edwin's playmate." She reached for a cloth doll with long yellow braids. "She's very changeable though." Flipping the doll, she revealed a second one, an old-fashioned Aunt Jemima, hidden among its full skirts. "And then there's Bruno. He gets in on the fun, too."

She gestured at a stuffed German shepherd standing nearby. For a few seconds I couldn't take my eyes from it. What a terrible thing to do to a pet!

Joan must have sensed my squeamishness. "Yeah, I would

have buried him, too. But you get used to him." Her voice had lost much of its animation, as if she'd wearied of her act. "What can I do for you?"

"Hank Zahn sent me over. From All Souls Legal Cooperative. He said you need some investigative work done."

"Oh, you're Sharon McCone!" She shook her head, laughing softly. "And here I was, giving you a sales pitch!"

"It was pretty effective. In a few minutes you could have sold me anything in the shop."

"That's good to know. Have a seat, why don't you." She gestured at a nearby chair. "I spoke to Hank on behalf of our Merchants' Association, which I'm a member of. All Souls has been handling my legal work and . . . oh, excuse me."

A remarkable-looking woman had come into the shop. She was tall, and her fine cascade of blond hair fell to her shoulders from under a brown suede hat with a long pheasant feather. Her face was well made up, classically beautiful; and her entire outfit was of suede like the hat, even to laced knee-high boots.

As if she sensed a sale here, Joan moved in quickly. "Good afternoon, ma'am. You look like you might enjoy meeting a lovely lady . . . "

I sat there for a minute as she drew the newcomer along on the same fantasy trip she'd taken me, modified here and there when she pointed out different objects of interest. Finally I got up and wandered around the shop, finding a couple of Oriental lamps and a carved table that would be perfect for my apartment. I was considering a black lacquered trunk with brass trimmings and a price very much out of my range when Joan Albritton called out to me.

"Okay, she's gone. Now you and I can talk business."

Reluctantly, I returned to the front. "She buy anything?"

"Sure, but frankly I thought she'd be more of a sale than she was."

"Oh, not so good?"

"Not bad, forty bucks. That Italian painting I showed you. Now I'll have to find Edwin a new picture to appreciate."

30

Then we had sat down and launched into a discussion of the vandals who had been plaguing Salem Street. It occurred to me, with a pang, as I came back to the present, that had I been more successful in my investigation, Joan might be here today, introducing still another unsuspecting stranger to the lovelorn lady from Paris.

Suddenly there was a tap on the door. Charlie Cornish. I went to let him in.

He entered the shop cautiously, keeping his eyes averted from the floor where Joan's body had lain. "Thought I'd stop in and see how you're doing."

"I'm not doing much. Right now the thought of the inventory intimidates me."

Charlie sat down on a stool by the counter. "I take it you don't know anything about antiques."

"Not a thing."

He nodded. "Let me warn you then: the hard part is telling the real ones from the others."

"The others?"

"Sure. Joanie had some good pieces here, damn good, but she ordered a lot through van Osten's catalogues, too."

"I know she bought things from him, but what do you mean?"

Charlie assumed a mock-pedagogical stance. "Well, consider how many antique stores there are in this city. Couple of hundred, right?"

"I guess so."

"Take my word for it. There are close to five pages of them in the phone book. Now, multiply that by all the other cities around the country. See what I mean?"

"I'm getting the drift."

"Good. Now, how many antiques are there to go around? Lately, the trend is for dealers to order stock from Europe, through catalogues. But Europe has only so many antiques, too."

"Are you saying the antiques are fake?"

"Oh, the catalogues claim they're the real article. But

31

when a big dealer or a department store orders fifty of number SS173X, oak washstand with marble inlay, how many of those washstands do you think the European catalogue house found sitting around in somebody's barn?"

"Not fifty, at any rate."

Charlie bestowed a proud glance on me. At this rate, I was going to go to the head of the class.

"Now," he went on, "if you think of them as products of an assembly-line process, that makes it more believable, right?"

"So most of this stuff," I gestured around the store, "is fraudulent?"

He winced a little. "That's kind of harsh. Let's face it, we're not any of us big-name dealers down here. Mostly the people who come to Salem Street are looking for something cheap to fill space in their apartments. Or, if they have a little extra to spend, they want a conversation piece. They're none of them collectors, and they don't demand authentication on what they buy. A lot of them are tourists who want to take a souvenir of their trip to San Francisco—maybe something like a lacquered Oriental vase—back home to the Midwest."

"And?"

"And it gives them the chance to poke around down here and have some fun buying that vase. It doesn't matter that it's the same thing they could have bought in Chinatown, 'cause hunting around Salem Street isn't as plastic as shopping in Chinatown. Sure, a lot of these so-called antiques are mass-produced, but Joanie and the others would have been the first to admit it, had anyone asked them."

I hadn't meant to put him on the defensive. Quickly I asked, "So they're all ordered from catalogues?"

"Right. Oliver van Osten acts as a broker for several European antique manufacturers." Charlie smiled at the contradiction in terms. "He comes around once a month and takes orders."

"He sells to a lot of people on the street?"

"To Joanie, Austin Bigby, maybe five or six others. He even helps them coordinate what they buy so they don't all end up with the same stock. It would look pretty funny if that same marble inlaid washstand turned up in every shop on the street!"

I grimaced sympathetically, trying to imagine the dealers explaining their way out of that. "Can you show me one of the fakes?"

"Sure." Charlie got up and went over to what looked like a little pedestal table. "This is a smoking stand. Carved pedestal, light ornamentation, copper-lined. Circa nineteen hundred. Now come with me."

He went toward the little workroom at the back, motioning for me to follow. The room was stacked with furniture, furniture I'd assumed needed refinishing or repairs before it was salable. In the corner, behind the littered workbench, Charlie pointed out three more smoking stands, identical to the first in every detail.

"Joanie bought five; that's about a standard order for large pieces. She sold one, and as soon as the customer left the shop, its twin was out on the floor."

I shook my head. "It still sounds underhanded to me."

"You're probably right, but that's the way it's done."

We returned to the main room and took up our former positions by the cash register.

I asked, "This van Osten, what do you know about him?"

"About Ollie?" Charlie shrugged. "He's a damned good salesman."

I was aware of that. "He must make a lot of money. I mean, he dresses well and drives an expensive car."

"Money is the prime motivation for any good salesman, and Ollie's a real success story."

"Tell me about him. What's his background?"

"Well, once when I got him talking, he told me he grew up in North Dakota—Fargo, to be exact. His father owned a tavern. Ollie ran away and joined the army as soon as he could, to get out of working in the bar. The army sent him to

Europe, he got interested in art, and stayed on to study. Now he's one of the most successful brokers in the country. Covers five states."

"Strange he'd go from studying art to selling fakes."

Charlie shook his head. "Not if you know Ollie. He found out there wasn't enough money in art, and so . . ."

"I see. You realize he hates for you to call him 'Ollie,' don't you?"

Charlie's grin was sly. "Of course. That's why I do it. But don't tell me you suspect Ollie?"

"I suspect anyone who was associated with Joan in any way."

The grin dropped off his face, and he flinched.

"Oh, Charlie, I didn't mean *you*." As I said it, I wondered why the big junkman *wasn't* on my list of suspects. "You cared for her, I know."

"A lot of people did. The street's not going to be the same without her." Charlie gazed into the shadows, as if he expected Joan Albritton to emerge from one of the aisles and make everything all right again.

"Of course," he added, "it's never going to be the same anyway. Come May first, we'll all go our separate ways, to wherever we can find new space."

"Have you found any?"

He gestured wearily. "Austin Bigby and I are going in together on a place over on Valencia Street. It's got lots of room, and the combination of my junk and his antiques should have good drawing power. But, damn it all, it'll never have the atmosphere we had here!" He looked as if he were about to cry.

Briskly I said, "At least you have good offers to pick from."

He nodded. "The Ingalls real-estate syndicate is bidding the most. They want to develop this into shops and condominiums."

"What's Cara Ingalls like anyway?" I had heard she was a power behind many of the large real-estate deals in the city,

34

and she interested me, since women didn't generally get in on the big operations.

"Don't know. I noticed her name in the business section of the paper this morning; that might tell you something. Why don't you come over and take a look at it?"

I could use all the background I could get on the people I wanted to talk to, so I locked up and followed Charlie across the street.

The article wasn't too informative. It said that Ingalls was to give a speech at a cocktail party for supporters of the Yerba Buena Convention Center at the Bank of America building this evening. The convention center, a controversial issue for years, had been repeatedly stalled by suits and counter-suits. In the meantime, south of Market Street, where buildings had been razed to clear the way for the new construction, land stood abandoned or turned into commuter parking lots. The party was at six o'clock in the Carnelian Room.

"Tell you anything interesting?" Charlie asked. He sat, as he always did on rainy days like today, chair leaning against the old office desk.

"A little."

"So what're you up to now?"

"I've got to get some library books on antiques, then go home and get dressed. I'm going to a cocktail party this evening."

# Six

At six o'clock that evening, I crossed the wind-swept plaza in front of Bank of America's world headquarters. A flower stand at the corner of Kearny and California added gaiety to the scene, but its early spring daffodils were offset by a nearby sculpture, known locally as "the banker's heart," which resembled a huge lump of coal.

I passed through the towering lobby of the building to the elevator that took me to the Carnelian Room. When I stepped off at the top floor, an eager young man in a brown double-knit suit greeted me.

"Good evening, ma'am. Step right over here, and I'll find your name tag and give you your Yerba Buena Supporter's Kit."

So this was a closed party. I followed him to a card table stacked with colorful folders and tags encased in plastic.

"Your name and organization?" he asked with an ingratiating smile.

"Sharon McCone, Wakefield and Fox," I said, naming one of the larger real-estate firms in the Bay Area.

He rummaged around on the table. "Oh, not again! They

37

don't seem to have made up your tag. You know how everything gets screwed up with these big parties." He produced a felt-tip pen and wrote my name and company on a card, then popped it into an empty sheath of clear plastic. "Let me help you pin it on."

In a few seconds, Sharon McCone, realtor, entered the Carnelian Room, clutching her Yerba Buena Supporter's Kit.

I accepted a drink from the first tray that passed, shifted the kit to my other arm so it covered my name tag, and wandered around the room.

People clustered in little groups, gesturing and talking with animation. I checked out the nearest bunch for Wakefield and Fox employees and, when I didn't find any, slipped onto its fringes, catching bits of the conversation.

". . . horrible what they're doing . . ."

". . . loss of millions of dollars of income . . ."

". . . why, when I think of the jobs it could create . . ."

". . . damned eco-freaks . . ."

I wondered if any of them really cared what the others were saying, since they all seemed to talk at once.

"Don't you agree, dear?"

A portly man in a leisure suit that fitted him like a sausage casing nudged me and managed to spill a little of his drink on my foot.

"Excuse me?" I set my empty glass on a passing tray and picked off two fresh ones. I would need fortification to get through this.

"No matter how you look at it," he went on, ignoring me, "the fact is, this city is suffering, really suffering. . . ." He pitched into a long harangue about how San Francisco couldn't survive without a new sports arena and several thousand more hotel rooms to join the ones that already stood empty in these days of slack tourism. I nodded at appropriate intervals, half listening. Finally several people began tapping silver on glasses at the front of the room.

The man beside me broke off in mid-sentence and turned to look. "They're ready for the Ingalls speech," he said.

38

"Damned fine woman. Ought to have been a man." He punctuated this by chomping vigorously on an ice cube.

I moved to where I could glimpse a long table with a speaker's podium on it. A distinguished-looking fellow with white hair was trying to speak over the din. The noise settled gradually, and I heard him introduce ". . . one of our most active and dedicated supporters of Yerba Buena, Mrs. Cara Ingalls."

A stunning blond, who appeared to be in her mid-thirties, stepped out of the crowd and crossed in front of the table, going around to the podium. Her hair fell to her shoulders from under a soft green beret, and she wore a sleekly styled knit dress in the same shade. I stared at her, trying to remember where I'd seen Cara Ingalls before.

"Thank you. Thank you and good evening, fellow Yerba Buena supporters." Her voice was husky, and her full lips parted in a warm smile. I had seen that smile, too, and recently.

A hush fell over the room, and Cara Ingalls began to speak of the convention center and the serious obstacles that were preventing the development of the massive project. Ignoring the substance of her words, I studied her.

Ingalls was tall and slender, but her body gave the impression of well-toned muscles and strength. The classic loveliness of her face provided a sharp contrast to the determined, predatory set of her features as she spoke of the Yerba Buena Center. She was feline in a way that reminded me that not all cats are domestic; some are dangerous.

Then, something she said jarred my memory. Of course I had seen Ingalls before: in Joan's shop the previous October. Cara Ingalls was the woman who had come in during my first visit to the shop and bought the painting after being introduced to Clothilde and Edwin. So, unknown to Joan, one of the potential purchasers of her land had been checking it—and her—out. I was sure that was why Ingalls had come to the shop: she didn't look like the sort who would need, or want, to buy her antiques on Salem Street.

39

I wasn't surprised, having seen her, that Cara Ingalls had climbed to the top of a rough and demanding profession. I knew I wanted to find out more about the woman and talk to her in person, to ask her if she'd ever introduced herself to Joan Albritton after her syndicate made its offer. I also wanted to know, in light of Joan's death, if the offer still stood.

After Ingalls's speech ended, I started toward the front of the room, determined to get her attention, but she was quickly surrounded by a crowd, all of whom looked importunate and long-winded. I got out one of my cards and scribbled on it, "Very anxious to talk with you about the Albritton murder." If anything, that should get her attention. I handed the card to the distinguished-looking gentleman who had introduced Ingalls, telling him to make sure she got it.

As I waited, I had to step back to let some people by and, in doing so, bumped into someone. I dropped my bag and my Yerba Buena Supporter's Kit, and the man I'd stepped on bent to pick them up.

As he straightened, his eyes caught my name tag, and he smiled.

"Hi, comrade! I'm Bill Tilbury, San Mateo office."

Just what I needed, a fellow employee.

"Nice to meet you." I edged away.

Good old Bill was not to be put off. "Hey, what office are you with?"

I kept backing up. "Here in the city."

"You mean One Embarcadero?"

"Right."

"Wait a minute. You must work with Ron!" He tapped the shoulder of a little guy next to him. "Hey, Ron, here's Sharon McCone from your office!"

Ron turned to look at me. He had a receding hairline and a pinched face. His eyes fell to my name tag. "You're not from our office," he said accusingly.

Bill Tilbury frowned. "She said she was."

40

"One Embarcadero? Wakefield and Fox? She's kidding you." Ron came toward me. "Look, lady, what are you trying to pull?"

I stepped backwards toward the door to the elevators. "I don't know what you're talking about. I'm new. Possibly we haven't met yet."

He pursued me furiously. "Try again. If you were new, you would have been introduced at the Monday morning pep meeting. All new employees, even the file clerks, are introduced then. What's your game anyway?"

"No game." I flew backwards through the door, almost bowling over the young man in the double-knit suit.

"Hey, stop her!" Ron exclaimed. "She's probably a spy for the eco-freaks! Hell, she might even be a spy for the Indians! She looks like one, and she's wearing Indian jewelry!" He pointed at my beaten-silver-and-turquoise choker.

Before I could wonder what the Indians had to do with Yerba Buena, I saw an elevator full of people. Its doors were just beginning to close.

"Why did you let her in?" Ron was practically shaking the young fellow.

I aimed for the elevator.

"Oh, my God, I even made her a name tag!" The young man sounded as if he had let a KGB agent into a meeting of the National Security Council.

I slipped through the elevator doors right before they closed. The people in the car looked at me in surprise.

"My former boyfriend," I explained. "He harasses me because I make more in commissions than he does."

The man next to me grinned, and I heard a few chuckles from the back of the car. We rode the rest of the way in silence, and I beat a hasty retreat from the building. Before I got into any more trouble on the Salem Street Merchants' Association's account, I'd better check with Charlie Cornish to make sure they'd voted to hire me.

# Seven

On the way to Junk Emporium, I stopped at a pay phone and called Lt. Marcus for the medical examiner's report. When I reached him, he summarized it briefly.

Cause of death: multiple stab wounds to the heart. Defensive slash wound, right hand. So she had fought off her attacker.

Bruise on the left side of the face, inflicted before death, but fairly soon before. He had struck her.

Estimated time of death: between nine thirty P.M. and twelve thirty A.M., the closest they could narrow it down. That meant she had been dead at least an hour when Charlie found her.

The rest of the physical evidence said very little: the dimensions of the wounds roughly matched those of the remaining bone-handled knives, and the blood samples taken from the carpet matched both the type and the subtype of the deceased's. Fingerprint evidence was inconclusive, since the shop was a public place. The only prints on the curio cabinet were partials and appeared to be those of the murdered woman.

"Overall," Marcus admitted, "the physical evidence isn't helpful. Something'll turn up though. In the meantime, you can get back to your antiques."

His tone was needling and unkind. Back to my antiques, in my proper place. Damn it, why did Marcus go out of his way to annoy me? It was strange behavior for a high-ranking, professional cop, even given the traditional antagonism of his breed for private operatives.

When I pulled up to the curb in front of Junk Emporium, I sat in the car a minute, watching a lone drunk grope his way along the sidewalk, the bottle in its paper bag clutched to his chest. After he passed, I got out and locked the car.

The big front windows of the shop were dark, but I could see light coming from way in back, where Charlie lived. I pounded hard on the door, and after a bit heard shuffling footsteps. Charlie's haggard face peered out at me, and then the bolts and locks started to turn.

When I stepped through the door, the sharp odor of gin hit me. Charlie was drowning his sorrows, and they apparently were dying hard. He regarded me a moment with bleary eyes, his mouth hanging slack, then mumbled, "Oh, it's you."

He immediately turned and wandered away, leaving me in the open door. I shut it and locked up as best I could, then followed in his meandering wake down the wide central aisle. On either side, battered old pieces of furniture lined up ponderously, spectators at our absurd little parade.

"It's an ill wind, Sharon. It's an ill wind blowing through the world tonight." Involuntarily, I shuddered. The musty room and Charlie's mood, not surprisingly, were making me wish I'd waited till morning.

"Can you feel it, Sharon? Blowing like it'll never stop?" Charlie peered back at me, his gaze unsteady.

Just what I need, I thought. A morose drunk on my hands. "I can feel it, Charlie."

"It's been blowing for a long time. I should of paid attention to it. Maybe it wouldn't of ended that way, not the way it did." His enunciation was remarkably clear, even if his eyes weren't focused.

I went up and took his arm. "Let's go in back and sit down, Charlie." I began steering him toward the source of the light. For a big man he felt surprisingly frail tonight.

"Loved her," he said huskily, leaning on me. "Everybody did." He then jerked away from me and whipped into brisk motion. "Come on and meet my friend. He loved her, too. I oughtn't of been so goddamn selfish, trying to keep her to myself."

It was too quiet for anyone else to be in the shop. My lord, I thought, now he's imagining things.

It was so quiet, in fact, that when a man appeared in the doorway in front of us, I jumped.

He was a tall man, taller than Charlie, with slightly rounded shoulders, and he wore a flashy tan suit. His bald head was surrounded by a ruff of brown hair, and the light from a floor lamp just inside the door gleamed off his thick horn-rimmed glasses and highlighted the heavy features of his face.

"Didn't mean to startle you," the man said in apologetic tones. "I'm Ben Harmon."

The name was vaguely familiar. I said, "Sharon McCone."

He smiled and held out a large, neatly manicured hand. "Oh, you're All Souls' investigator. I've heard a lot about you, from Joan."

His words made me remember how I knew his name. Ben Harmon, bail bondsman. He was the man who had originally sent Joan to All Souls when her grandson had been arrested for possession of narcotics. His office was a few blocks away, on Bryant Street. Joan, unable to cope when she got news of the arrest, had turned to him for help.

Harmon had a reputation for rough dealing, I recalled. If you were smart, you didn't even think of jumping bail on Ben Harmon. He employed a staff of men who were pros at tracking down fugitives, and anyone who violated his agree-

45

ment with Harmon was found and speedily dragged back to jail. I had heard about one case when Harmon's men had managed to retrieve a recalcitrant accused of murder who had fled to Mexico.

Now Charlie lunged through the doorway and extended his arm in the general direction of Ben Harmon's shoulders. "Want you to meet a good friend. And Joanie's good friend. Ben loved Joanie, too."

Harmon smiled tolerantly and extricated himself from the embrace. "Let's all sit down, Charlie. I'll get Miss McCone a drink."

Charlie nodded happily and lurched into a shabby over-stuffed chair. The little room was scantily furnished: it contained a small love seat, formica coffee table, battered bureau, and thin mattress on an iron bedstand. A couple of sets of fatigues and Charlie's old sheepskin jacket hung from pegs on the far wall. A second lamp, a cracked china base festooned with yellow roses, gave feeble light to the coffee table. The poverty of Charlie's life threatened to overwhelm me as I sat down on the lumpy love seat and had to move to avoid a protruding spring.

A cocktail shaker, with a corroding metal top, stood on the table next to several bottles of gin and vermouth. Harmon selected one of the glasses lined up there, inspecting it for cleanliness. It was smudged and clouded, like all the others.

He glanced at me with a helpless look, poured straight gin into the glass, and handed it to me with a little bow. Evidently Charlie's spree had begun with martinis, but that pretense at amenity had long since been abandoned.

I smiled ruefully in return and sipped a little of the gin, trying not to gag. Harmon sat down next to me on the love seat. I noticed another glass of the colorless liquid on the floor near his feet.

Harmon turned to me with a questioning look. "Are you investigating Joan's . . . ?"

Querulous words from Charlie interrupted him. "You did love her, didn't you, Ben, old Ben?"

"Everybody loved Joan," Harmon said evenly. "She and I were very good friends."

"You wouldn't of been if I'd been watching like I should of." Charlie was beginning to slur his words. "If I'd of been able to help her when the kid got picked up by the cops. She comes to me, says 'Charlie, what am I going to do?' But what was I supposedta say? I didn't know what to do either. Hell, I don't mess with drugs. What was I supposedta know?"

"You did right, Charlie," Harmon said soothingly.

"Shit! Sure I did. 'Go see Ben Harmon,' I says. 'He gets folks outa jail all the time.' So she did; and next thing you know, old Ben Harmon is around here, stopping in to see Joanie, hanging around her, helping her out when the stupid kid goes and O.D.'s. Good old Ben, moving in on my woman."

Harmon looked at me and frowned, then said, "Now, you know it wasn't like that, Charlie."

"Wasn't it? Wasn't it? Then what were you doing there? Why didn't you go home to your wife and kids and that palace you're always talking about out in the Sunset? What the hell were you doing with my woman? I should of been the one to comfort her. I always was until you. Wasn't it like that, Mr. High-and-Mighty Harmon?"

The bail bondsman kept his expression blank. "Charlie, you're going to feel a lot better in the morning. You're going to feel a lot better about everything and then we'll forget you ever said this."

"Feel better in the morning?" Charlie snorted loudly. "I'm not gonna feel better. I'm gonna feel like hell. I'll have the champion hangover of San Francisco. And it won't make me change my mind about you, old Ben."

Harmon stood up, tugging at his suit-coat. "I think you'll change your mind, Charlie. I think you will."

There was an undertone to his words that I couldn't understand. I wondered what the relationship was between the two men, besides their mutual interest in Joan Albritton.

47

Harmon straightened the knot of his paisley tie, regarding Charlie through his thick glasses. Now that the light no longer shone directly on them, I could see his eyes were brown but without the soft quality brown eyes usually have.

"You'll feel better soon," he said softly. He then turned to me and held out his hand again. "Nice meeting you, Miss McCone. Take care of our boy here." I started to get up to let him out, but he added, "No, don't bother. I'll go out the back way. The door self-locks."

He turned and left the room. Charlie followed him with his eyes, not moving his head.

"Harmon's a bastard," he muttered, more to himself than to me. "I tried to tell her. I tried."

I set the glass of gin down on the floor close to the love seat. "Look, Charlie, don't you think you should get some sleep?"

"Sleep?" He laughed mirthlessly. "I lay down, all I'm gonna get is the whirlies. You ever had the whirlies? Round and round . . ."

"Yes, I've had the whirlies. Everybody's had the whirlies. Charlie, what happened at the Merchants' Association meeting?" I was impatient to get the answer I'd come for.

"Oh, we took up a collection. Gonna get the biggest goddamn wreath for Joanie. You wanna contribute?" He leaned forward, holding out his hand.

I sighed inwardly and said, "How much should I?"

"Couple of bucks would do."

I reached for my bag and got out a five. "That's from me and Hank and the others at All Souls."

Charlie stared at the bill. "That's a lot. They don't pay you much. Can you afford it?"

"I'll make them pay back their shares out of petty cash."

Charlie kept staring at the bill. "Petty. That's what it was. I was petty. She'd of still been alive if I wasn't a petty bastard."

"How do you mean?" The night before, Charlie had lashed out at me for failing to unmask the vandals and thus prevent

48

Joan's death. Now I wondered if his attack on me had been an extension of some secret guilt of his own. If so, how much of that guilt was founded on fact?

Charlie said, "She wouldn't of been alone, that's what I mean. All alone with Old Father Death. If I hadn't of been so petty."

"I don't understand."

He looked up at me, a sly light in his tiny eyes. "She was alone and Old Father Death came creeping . . ."

I decided we were getting nowhere this way. "Charlie, what else happened at the meeting?"

He looked blank. "What?"

"Are they going to hire me?"

"Hire you?"

"The Merchants' Association! Do they want me to investigate the murder?"

"Oh, hire you. No. They voted against it, Sharon." An apologetic note crept into his voice. "I guess Joanie's death ended the Association. There's no feeling of togetherness any more. Joanie's gone, and nobody can bring her back."

I felt a disappointed twinge. "They don't want to find her killer?"

"Yes. No. I don't think anybody cares. We just all want out before it's one of us next." He glanced furtively over his shoulder. "You see, Old Father Death's lurking around Salem Street, and he's going to strike again. He could be out there in the dark right now. Who knows? I want out, too." There was a wild light in his eyes.

I shook my head, shivering. Charlie might be babbling drunk, but he raised spectres I couldn't deal with. "Stop talking like that, Charlie. Nobody else is going to die."

"I'm going to die. You're going to die. We all are. In our time, in our own special way. Who knows but that our time is now? Maybe it's there, just seconds away, out there . . ."

I stood up. "Look, Charlie, I've got to go. You better follow me out and make sure you lock up after me."

"You can go out the back way. It locks behind you."

49

"No," I said firmly. "My car's in front." Damned if I would go out into the alley with Charlie's Old Father Death lurking in the dark!

It was bad enough to pass through the roomful of junk on the way to the front door. Several times, I glanced from side to side but saw nothing more threatening than a huge, ugly armoire with gorgons carved on its doors. Just the same, I was glad to get out of there. I waited long enough to make sure Charlie shot the bolt, then raced for my car, fumbling with the keys.

I needed light, and reasonable, sober people to dispel the gloomy foreshadowing of my own uncertain death. I also needed to talk to Hank about the new turn of events. Could I investigate Joan's murder without the Merchants' Association's sponsorship? I wanted to investigate it very much.

I headed for All Souls to see Hank. If he was anything, it was reasonable and sober.

# *Eight*

My gloom was somewhat alleviated when I arrived at All Souls. The windows of the Victorian building glowed cheerfully, and the porch light spread a wide circle of welcome into the night. I took the front steps two at a time and hurried down the first-floor hallway, past the empty offices toward the sound of voices.

In the living room, I found several of the associates sprawled on the floor around a Monopoly board. The board was covered with little green houses and big red hotels, and a fortune in paper money lay scattered about.

"Hank?" I asked when the game players looked up to see who had come in.

One of them gestured toward the kitchen.

I kept going, following a long red cord that trailed on the floor. At its end, I found Hank, pacing back and forth with the telephone cradled in his arms. Red push-button phones with twenty-five-foot cords were a small, harmless fetish at

All Souls. There were seven extensions on the first floor alone, and their users habitually abandoned them wherever they were when they finished talking. Often the red cords got hopelessly snarled together, with the resulting mazes requiring expert attention.

"Listen, you have nothing to worry about. The old fool can't sue you; he has absolutely no grounds," Hank was saying. "And if I don't get back to what I was doing before you called, I stand to lose out on an option for some very choice real estate. Right. 'Bye." He clapped the receiver in place and smiled at me. "Boardwalk and Park Place are still up for grabs."

I sighed and said, "I hate to interrupt your wheeling and dealing, but I do need to talk with you."

He shrugged and said in mock sorrow, "I wasn't cut out to be an entrepreneur anyway. Let's go talk in the map room."

On the way out of the kitchen, I grabbed a handful of cookies from the big jar that was always full of chocolate chips. They would be my dinner. Hank grinned and led me down the central hall to the second office on the right.

The room was aptly named, since all four walls and part of the ceiling were covered with maps: a huge street map of San Francisco; Bay Area road maps, all spliced together and curling up on the floor; U.S. maps; maps showing popular hiking trails, campgrounds, congressional districts, wineries with tours and tasting, city bus routes, and postal zip codes. In addition, there was a highly useful collection of tide tables, airline schedules, and menus from carry-out restaurants.

Hank sat down behind the desk and gestured at the client's chair. "What can I do for you, ma'am?"

I quickly related the scene with Charlie and Ben Harmon, not going into my attack of the willies. Hank sat quietly, tapping a pencil on the desk while he listened.

"Interesting," he said when I was through. "So Ben Harmon was holding Charlie's hand, was he?"

"I wouldn't go so far as that. He let Charlie think they

52

were drinking together. What's your relationship with Harmon anyway? As I recall, he sent Joan to you."

Hank nodded. "Occasionally he refers a client to us, when he comes across someone for whom a legal services plan is appropriate. Harmon's a frustrated attorney himself and a bit of a courthouse hanger-on. Otherwise, we really don't have a relationship at all."

"He's kind of a rough character, isn't he?"

"He has that reputation, which is one reason I wouldn't want to see All Souls any more closely connected to him than it already is."

"What do you suppose his connection with Charlie is?"

Hank frowned. "Really couldn't say. It would be interesting to find out. They may have business dealings. Harmon does a lot of what he refers to as 'business on the side.' He likes to imagine himself a high roller, but in my opinion he's not smart enough for those circles. You know the type: always got a hot deal going but nothing ever comes of it.

"He has what he calls a 'syndicate,'" Hank went on. "All people that I would guess he's gathered solely on the basis of their ability to provide him with capital for his schemes. So if he asks you to invest in a treasure hunt or something, my advice is to hang on to your pennies."

I smiled. "Pennies is all I've got right now. Forgetting Harmon for the minute, I have another question for you. About Joan's estate: who inherits? Or was there even a will?"

"There's a will; I ought to know. It was like pulling teeth to get her to make one. You wouldn't believe the state Albritton kept her business affairs in. Just incredible! I don't know how she managed to squirrel away all the money she did, what with the messy way she operated."

"The estate is large then?"

"Substantial."

"And since she had no family, who does it go to?"

"I thought you'd realize," Hank said. "Charlie Cornish. He gets it all."

I hadn't realized, but now that he'd pointed it out, it was

logical. Logical and somewhat disturbing. After a minute, I said, "Well, in light of the Salem Street merchants not backing me, there's not much I can do about the murder but work on that inventory and keep my eyes open. Maybe I can drag the inventory out to give myself more time."

"Don't take too much. Greg Marcus is well aware of my reason for having you hang around the shop. I don't want to abuse the privilege and destroy his cooperative mood."

The mention of Marcus annoyed me. "He doesn't strike me as so cooperative. He's only allowing it as a favor to you, and he acts as if he were sure I wouldn't find out anything of value anyway." The lieutenant's comment about getting back to my antiques still irked me.

"Now don't go sticking out your chin and getting belligerent on me," Hank said. "You know, you've developed a funny attitude toward the worthy lieutenant. I'd say you were interested in him, the way you get perturbed every time his name comes up."

I sniffed haughtily. "That's hardly the case. I prefer my men to be sensitive."

"Like that rock musician you were going with down south?" Hank loved to tease me about my private life.

"Besides being a rock musician, John's a very talented pianist. Anyway, that's kind of tapered off."

Hank frowned. "What happened?"

"Nothing. But when you live two hundred and fifty miles apart and see each other twice a year, if you're lucky, eventually you have to admit the relationship's cooled down. I'll always care about John, though."

"So now you're looking."

"You make it sound like the big safari is on. Sure, I'm open to possibilities, but I'm not about to start prowling the singles bars. I don't have to be romantically involved with someone to feel complete, and certainly a woman would be desperate to turn to Greg Marcus for companionship!"

Hank grunted. "Don't be too sure. Greg's been married once, to a hell of a good woman; and a few years ago, he was the unnamed correspondent in a society divorce. He's what you might call 'a wolf in a misogynist's clothing.' "

"Well, to mix metaphors, I don't hear the call of the wild. Besides, I notice the wife didn't stick around."

"Then your feelings toward him must be solely competitive."

"What's that supposed to mean?"

"Let's face it. I know you. I bet the picture of Greg's having to admit you'd caught up with the killer before he did is a pretty gratifying one."

"So what's wrong with a little healthy competition?" I asked. "It'd do Marcus good."

Hank laughed. "Wait till I tell him that!"

"You wouldn't. It would spoil the surprise for him."

"You're right, I won't. But I want *you* to get the inventory done as your first priority. Any one-upmanship with the lieutenant can wait until that's taken care of."

I stood up and said, "All right, you're the boss. But I think it's a pretty poor use of a trained investigator to have me sit there and count bric-a-brac while a killer's on the loose."

I turned to go then, leaving him to think on my words while I made a dignified exit, but I only succeeded in hooking the strap of my shoulder bag on the arm of the chair. I turned back and wrenched it free, glaring. Hank's eyes were quietly amused.

"Hey, Shar," he said.

"What?" The word came out a rude snarl that embarrassed me.

"I think you've met your match in Greg Marcus."

"Oh, do you now? Well, it works both ways. Maybe he's met his match in me!"

I marched out of the office, careful not to slam the door. Behind it, I could hear Hank laughing.

Well, Hank wanted the goddamn bric-a-brac counted soon, so that was what he'd get. In fact, I'd start tonight.

# Nine

The highboy, I thought, had to be Queen Anne. Or was it Chippendale? Which one of them had those funny feet? Because this highboy had funny feet, very funny feet indeed. I stared at the illustrations in one of the antique collector's guides I'd borrowed from the library, then leaned my head against the offending object. My watch showed three fifteen in the morning, and I was exhausted.

I could go home, but it didn't seem worth the effort, so I found an afghan on a chair near the cash register, wrapped myself in it, and curled up all five-foot-six-inches of me on the mauve settee, next to Clothilde.

"It's a good thing I'm not superstitious," I told the dressmaker's form, "because I'm sure there must be something about it being bad luck to sleep in a room where a murder's been done. But you and I know better, don't we, old girl?"

It then occurred to me that I ought to ask Clothilde what

she had seen the night of the murder. Of course, she wouldn't have any answer, having no head and thus no eyes.

Sharon McCone, you are going insane, I thought, as I twisted around to find a comfortable position on the little settee.

Maybe it was trying to sleep like that in an unfamiliar place, or maybe I really did harbor eerie feelings about the scene of a violent death, but I couldn't doze off. I would be aware, terribly aware, that I was almost asleep, and then the awareness would jerk me completely awake. My body twitched, and I sat up several times with the sensation of falling. When I began to hear strange sounds and think how isolated I was, surrounded by abandoned, burned-out buildings, I became thoroughly disgusted with myself and started counting backwards from one thousand. It worked, as it always did, around seven hundred and fifty.

Then I dreamed, a great Technicolor dream, of chasing Edwin, the iron-shod mannequin, down into a labyrinth, which opened in the antique shop floor. He ran, feet clanking, eluding me. The labyrinth was draped with macramé cobwebs, and I tried to avoid them by weaving from side to side, but it didn't help. One of the cobwebs brushed my face with an evil, mocking caress. I screamed in terror.

And sat straight up on the settee, safely back in the antique shop. But I was not alone. Someone else was in the shop, someone who had brushed by me and was now moving toward the workroom and the back door.

Throwing off the afghan, I leaped up and tore into the workroom after him, not stopping to think what to do if I caught him. On the way, I grabbed up a hammer from the edge of the workbench and kept going, suddenly colliding with a dark figure.

I raised the hammer, but the intruder spun and grabbed me. The impact made the hammer fly through the air, and in one swift motion, I followed it, spinning along and crashing to the floor on my side, on top of what I later discovered to be a genuine fake umbrella rack, circa nineteen ten. Free of me, the intruder wrenched the door open and fled, his footsteps racing down the alley.

I lay on the floor for a minute. My breath came hard, and my eyes filled with tears of pain. Finally, I got up and turned on the light to see what damage I'd done. There was a long scrape on my left arm, and I knew bruises would soon show on my leg, but otherwise I seemed okay. The flimsy umbrella rack was wrecked.

There was, or had been, something in the shop that mattered enough for someone to pick a lock in a dark alley at four thirty in the morning. Someone? Who? Certainly not Charlie's Old Father Death. *He* didn't need to pick locks.

I shut and secured the door, then cleared the remaining antiques away from it so they wouldn't present obstacles to pursuit if the intruder returned. If he did, I'd have him, but I was betting he wouldn't be back. When I finished, I went into the front room, debating whether to curl up on the settee again or do the sensible thing and go home. I was still badly shaken, and I realized that this dilapidated building was a dangerous place to be in the middle of the night, when Salem Street was deserted. Certainly it had been fatal for Joan Albritton.

In a quiet panic, I gathered up my bag and jacket but froze in mid-flight. The sound of crashing glass rang out in the street, and I dropped to the floor. It took a couple more crashes for me to realize that my building was not the one under siege. I crept foward as still more noise shattered the air, and raised up to peer over the window sill at the street.

In the light from the corner lamppost, I saw the smashed glass front of Junk Emporium. In a moment, Charlie came flying out the door and looked wildly in both directions. He stood for a few seconds amidst the rubble on the sidewalk, then leaned down and picked up what looked like a brick.

So the vandalism was starting again.

Still trembling, I went to the door, unlocked it, and stepped out into the street. All was quiet now, except for Charlie's vigorous cursing. I started across to him, then whirled, a tremor passing along my spine. I had left the shop door open, an invitation for someone to slip through it, the same someone who had broken in while I slept. Suppose he hadn't had time to get what he wanted before I woke screaming? I quickly retraced my steps.

Could that possibly have been the purpose of the brick throwing, I wondered? Had the would-be burglar thought he could decoy me from the shop by attacking Junk Emporium? If so, he'd almost succeeded.

And what had I seen in the street at the moment I brought my eyes level with the window sill? I had not really seen, so much as had an impression of, a short, stocky figure running down the sidewalk and merging with the shadows. It could have been the same figure I'd tangled with minutes before.

My heart pounded as I returned to the settee and huddled in the afghan, longing for my warm, comfortable bed and the double lock and chain on my apartment door. But it was out of the question to go home now. If the intruder hadn't gotten what he wanted, it was my business to stay and protect the shop. At least I could take encouragement from the fact that he had pushed me away rather than attacked me when I came after him.

For the first time since the night before, when I'd seen the bloodstains and the chalk marks vividly outlining the tragedy that had befallen the little antique dealer, Joan's murder became intimate and horrible to me, with Charlie's Old Father Death returning to stalk my mind once more.

I sat, cocooned, leaning against Clothilde for comfort as I waited for the morning light.

# Ten

The light came, but slowly. I found I could doze off once my first attack of dread ended, and at full dawn I lapsed into a deep sleep that, while not long, refreshed me. Around nine o'clock, I woke to the sound of hammering in the street.

I went to the window and looked out at a soft, drizzling rain. Across the way, Charlie was hard at work nailing plywood sections over the holes in the glass front of his shop. The rain fell on him, dampening his long gray mane.

I sighed, depressed by the gloom, and went into the little bathroom at the back of the shop to tidy up. I smoothed the wrinkles out of my rumpled clothing as well as I could and tied my hair back so it wouldn't get in the way while I continued my crawl through the dusty depths of the selling floor and workroom. Then I fished in my bag for one of the Hershey bars I always carried with me and had breakfast.

The shop had soaked up some of the moisture from outside. I turned the heat on full blast, pushed up my sleeves, and with the inventory sheets in hand, began where I'd left off the night before. I was determined to get on with this task and test out a theory I'd formulated while I sat shivering in the dark.

It seemed to me that the intruder could be one of two people: a real burglar who knew the owner was dead and had decided to help himself to the contents of the shop, or Joan Albritton's murderer. And, if it was the murderer, he had returned for whatever he had left or neglected to take with him the night before. If I could discover what that something was, I might be able to identify the killer. I pursued the inventory furiously.

About an hour later, I was creeping on my hands and knees under a gate-leg table, trying to look at a pewter tea service that for some inexplicable reason had been hidden there, when I heard the front door open and quick footsteps cross the shop.

"Who's there?" I called.

The footsteps stopped. "Where are you?" a male voice asked.

I started to get up, hit my head on the underside of the table, and said, "Damn it!" in a very loud voice. I must have been making an interesting impression on whoever was out there.

He chuckled, and then a pair of shoes appeared next to the table. A hand reached under to help me out, and I took it, emerging dust-covered and red-faced. It was Oliver van Osten. I had forgotten about his promise to stop by and help me take inventory.

Van Osten looked well scrubbed and tidy. I hastily rubbed my dirty hands on my pants, until it occurred to me what a slovenly thing that was to do. Van Osten didn't seem to notice, though; he merely smiled and asked, "How are you doing?"

"Pretty well, but there's so much stuff here. Even knowing some of the antiques aren't genuine, it's still kind of overwhelming."

He nodded. "That's where I can help you. Let's sit down,

and I'll tell you a few things about antiques, to demystify them, so to speak."

I led him to the front of the room. Van Osten sat down next to Clothilde, patting the mannequin's shoulder in a proprietary fashion. I perched on a high stool behind the counter.

"How's your murder investigation going?" Van Osten asked.

"Better than the inventory," I lied.

"Any suspects?"

"None that I can discuss right now."

Van Osten furrowed his brow in displeasure at that.

"How well did you know Joan Albritton, Oliver?" I asked.

The furrow deepened. "Not well. She was just a customer, although I must say she was better than most."

"How so?"

"She knew something about antiques, about art." He made a scornful gesture. "Most of the buyers, what do they know? I could pass my 'antiques' off as the real article, and they'd never see the difference."

"They're that unaware of what they sell?"

"You'd be surprised at their ignorance. In private life, some of them are collectors; I advise them on artworks to buy. They don't care what it is, so long as it has an impressive price tag." His face twisted into a sneer. "They have to ask me what to buy, and then they treat me as if I should come in through the service entrance! Take a look around, and you'll find peasants in some pretty high places!"

Van Osten was exhibiting what appeared to be the paranoia of the former small-town boy made to feel small again. I said, "You must know a great deal about art."

"Enough," he said shortly. "I've studied under some of the great authorities. But let's get back to the facts you'll need for this inventory."

I sensed he realized he'd shown too much of himself to me. I nodded. "Okay. What can you tell me?"

Van Osten relaxed, secure in his role as teacher. "Number one: a lot of the impressive labels or catchwords you hear

63

applied to antiques are simply the dealer's jargon, and their purpose is largely to keep prices up."

"How so?"

Van Osten gestured at a shelf behind me. "Take a look at that urn up there. If Joan spotted a customer eying it, she'd probably strike up a conversation, call it a 'distinguished aging receptacle,' and make a sale. Now, you and I know it's nothing more than an old pickle crock, but as an 'aging receptacle,' it's got considerably more financial clout."

I got his point.

"Dealers like to upgrade their wares with grandiose descriptions," van Osten went on. "They'll make statements like 'It's in the style of Louis the Fourteenth,' but that doesn't mean it's ever been any closer to France than across the Bay Bridge. And when you get down to it, most of the stuff you'll find on Salem Street is in the style of the old pickle crock, if it's got any style at all."

I said, "You make it sound a very tricky business."

"Sure. It is." He got up and went to the curio cabinet, which still stood open, and extracted a small oblong box. "What do you think this is?"

"A pill box?"

"Wrong! It's a snuff box. They used to be all the rage. There's a whole ritual to it. Tap the box three times, no more or no less, to settle the snuff. Open it, pinch just so . . ." He mimicked the procedure, taking some imaginary snuff.

"Now, this box," he said, extending it to me, "is made of wood, and it's old enough but of rather humble American origins. I'm willing to bet you, though, that Joan Albritton could have convinced an unsophisticated buyer that this box could be 'attributed to' Napoleon's imperial tobacconist. The statement would be true in a way, but Joan would have been the only one doing the attributing."

I could believe that, having seen her at work.

"So you see," van Osten concluded, "you really have nothing to be afraid of. Once I've pointed out the pieces I sold to Joan, the remainder will all fall into place."

"You make it sound so simple."

"That's what I'm here for. I'll also be glad to go over Joan's records with you. They should indicate what values to assign to the genuine pieces."

I hesitated. Van Osten didn't strike me as a man who would be helpful unless there was something in it for him. In spite of what he'd said the morning before, he wasn't here because he'd always had a desire to be Ellery Queen.

I said, "All right. When I find the records—if there even are any—we'll go over them." I got off the stool slowly. "Right now you can show me the things Joan bought from you, and I'll tag them."

Three hours later we were almost done. Joan had bought all sorts of things through van Osten, from candlesticks to hall chairs, from miniatures to silver plate. He also told me the right names for many of the genuine pieces, so I only needed to match them with the record of the price Joan had paid. He would be hard-pressed however, van Osten said, to place a value on Clothilde, Edwin, or Bruno.

"Joan was extremely attached to them for some reason." He was standing in front of Edwin, the heavy-footed mannequin. "I think she half-believed they could hear her talking to them. I've often felt Joan would have made a great disciple of some pagan religion, with her tendency to imbue inanimate objects with life qualities."

He paused, reaching for the painting on Edwin's wall. "And this obsession with giving him something to look at. I could swear Edwin was a substitute for that grandson of hers who died. She developed the Edwin mania at about that time."

"Is that one of your paintings?" I asked, gesturing at the Madonna in his hands.

He glanced at it. "No. It's probably locally done. There are a number of competent copy artists around town."

I took it from him and looked at it. "I have a friend who would probably know who did it. Maybe I'll ask her to take a look at all the unidentified paintings here. I notice there are a few."

Van Osten frowned. "I'd give them a blanket value of five

bucks apiece if I were you, and save your friend the trouble. In fact, I'll give you five for that one right now. I have a crack in my bathroom wall that needs covering."

I laughed and said, "If I were allowed to conduct business, I'd probably take you up on it." I hung the painting back on the wall and led him down the last aisle, making notes on my inventory sheets and attaching tags. The whole process took only fifteen minutes more.

When we were done, van Osten put his coat on and got ready to leave, giving me his card in case I had further questions and reminding me to get in touch when I had located Joan's records.

I said I would, and we shook hands solemnly. Then I followed him to the door to say good-bye. Behind him, parked at the curb, was a black vehicle that practically shouted "unmarked police car." And as van Osten walked off, Lt. Marcus got out and came toward me.

# *Eleven*

I stood in the doorway of the shop, watching Greg Marcus cross the sidewalk. His usual sarcastic expression was in place by the time he got to the door: the familiar mocking quirk of the mouth, one dark-blond eyebrow raised.

"I see you're hard at work," he said. "Who's your friend?" He gestured down the street after van Osten.

"An antique dealer. He's been giving me pointers." I turned and went inside. Marcus followed.

"How're you getting along anyway?" he asked, draping his damp raincoat over the back of a chair.

"As well as can be expected. Please don't leave your coat there. It's Early American, and the water will spoil the finish." Much as I didn't give a damn about the antiques per se, Marcus's carelessness irritated me.

He looked at me in exaggerated surprise, then picked up the coat, ostentatiously wiping a few drops of water from the chair. "Jesus, we wouldn't want to damage one of these valuable antiques, would we?"

"Not that particular one. It's genuine, and there are very few other things of any real value in this shop." I turned away from him toward the stool by the cash register.

Marcus's voice came over my shoulder. "Yes, papoose, I can see you're learning a lot. It's a pity it hasn't improved your temper—or your appearance, for that matter. You look like you could use a bath."

I whirled around. "What's this 'papoose' bit?"

"That's what they call little Indians, isn't it? Or would you rather I called you 'squaw'?"

I was shaking with anger, but I kept my voice level. "You have no business calling me either. I don't have to listen to your comments on my ancestry or on the way I look. I can imagine you wouldn't look so great yourself if you'd spent the night on that couch."

He glanced at Clothilde's settee, then sat down. Unlike van Osten, he gave the dressmaker's form an uncomfortable look and edged away from her.

"You're right. I'd look like hell if I'd slept on this." He took out a cigarette, lit it, and stuck the match in a pewter bowl.

I snatched the bowl out of his reach and, with a gesture that mimicked his wiping the chair, transferred the match to a utilitarian glass ashtray.

Marcus watched me with narrowed eyes. "Sorry," he said. "I should have known that was valuable too, but I'm not the expert you are."

"It doesn't take expertise to see it's not an ashtray." I went over and perched on the stool. When I looked at him again, Marcus was staring at me with a peculiar expression.

"You spent the night here?" he asked. "In this room, where the body was found?"

At least he had stopped baiting me, for the moment. "I was working late, and it seemed silly to go home."

"Jesus," he muttered, shaking his head.

His reaction almost made my panic and restless dreams

worthwhile. "Well, the body was gone, wasn't it? Besides, a couple of interesting things happened."

"Oh?" He leaned forward on the settee.

"Someone broke in here early this morning. I chased him and we scuffled, but he got away. Right after that, someone smashed the front windows of Charlie Cornish's shop."

"I noticed he had them boarded up." Marcus looked thoughtful. "Did you get a good look at the person who broke in?"

"No."

"How long between the break-in and the smashed windows?"

"Maybe five minutes."

"See anyone then?"

"I had an impression, size and shape."

"What kind of impression?"

"Short to medium height. Stocky. Like the man who broke in here."

He snorted. "Like about a third of the men in this city."

"I didn't say I could describe him. What's important is he may have tried to decoy me away from the shop by breaking those windows."

"Why do you think that?"

"It's logical."

"Sounds more like a woman's intuition than logic."

I shifted on the stool and started fiddling with my hair, as I always did when angered. My fingers tangled in the ribbon, and I jerked it out savagely, letting my hair fall to my shoulders. Why did Marcus feel he must oppose everything I said?

Keeping my voice calm, I said, "I still think that's what happened."

"So what do you think this person wanted?"

"I've been trying to figure that out all morning. It was either something he left behind or something he forgot to take the night before. What, I don't know."

"Oh?" The mocking eyebrow trick again. "So you think this individual was the murderer?"

69

"Yes, I do."

"This 'he'... ever consider it might have been a she? Women commit murder, too."

"Don't I know!" I retorted beneath my breath, but Marcus caught it and gave me his pseudo-smile.

Returning the smile, I asked disingenuously, "What about you? What have you done that's interesting?"

He glared at me and ground out his cigarette in the ashtray. "The possible suspects you mentioned in your statement check out clean."

"The credit union people?"

"Them, and the people with the free school—they've bought land elsewhere, so they're out of the running. I agree with you about the law school and the Ingalls real-estate syndicate. That leaves us with the people here in the neighborhood."

"Wait a minute. Did your men talk with Mrs. Ingalls or the Hemphill Law School trustees?"

He looked annoyed. "They will, if they haven't already, but it's strictly routine. There's no reason to suspect any of them, and I'd hardly want to bother such people over this murder."

I reflected his annoyance back at him. "Why not? Are they so much better than Joan Albritton? Can't you take a few minutes of their precious time to try to find out who killed her?"

"Now, Sharon," he said in a patronizing tone, "I agreed with your opinion. I've only so much time to waste on false leads, and I prefer to concentrate here, in the neighborhood."

"That's the second time you've mentioned 'the neighborhood.' Is it a euphemism for someone you suspect?"

"Could be. I hoped you'd cooperate. Are you going to be obstructive now?"

I got down from the stool and began pacing up and down behind the counter.

Finally I said, "I don't understand you. Is there some pressure from higher up that makes you reluctant to interrogate people in this city's so-called power structure? Or is it

70

that you've got one idea in your head, and you're closing your eyes to all other possibilities?"

As soon as I said it, I wished I'd phrased it more tactfully. Marcus went rigid, and for a moment he didn't speak. Then he leaned forward and said in a hard voice, "Watch it, Ms. McCone. You're here only because I say so, you know."

"My boss was Joan Albritton's attorney, and this inventory is within the scope of my duties."

"I said, watch it. You have an unusual interest in this murder. If Zahn didn't vouch for you, I'd say you were protecting someone."

I stared at him. "Who do you have in mind?"

"This Cornish fellow, for one. I understand you're pretty chummy with him, paid him a visit last night."

His words brought me up short. After a few seconds, I asked, "Are you having me followed?"

"Of course not. But I have my sources." He got up and stood across the counter from me, looking smug.

"I have a right to visit anyone I want to." My voice shook with rage.

"Not if you're obstructing a police investigation, you don't."

I stood, staring at him, unable to speak. Marcus's glance moved from my face, down my body, to my hands. I looked down, too. My angry fingers had fashioned the hair ribbon I was clutching into a little noose.

Marcus's eyes traveled slowly back to my face. "You aren't too good at covering up your emotions, are you?" He paused, then leaned closer, his face set. "Now, I have something to tell you, Ms. McCone, and I want you to listen carefully. You have forty-eight hours, exactly, to finish this inventory and get out of the shop. By noon, day after tomorrow, you are to be gone.

"If I see or hear of you talking to anyone involved with the case, if you harass anyone, like the Hemphill people or Mrs. Ingalls, I'll see that you never work again in any investigatory capacity. You will go back to guarding dresses in department stores, where, in my opinion, you belong!"

I took a step backwards, still speechless.

"In addition," Marcus went on, "I'm putting a twenty-four-hour guard on this building, in case your so-called murderer returns. I don't want it on my head if you get yourself stabbed to death while inventorying this trash."

He had ridiculed my suggestion that the intruder and the killer were the same person, but he thought it important enough to put a man on the shop.

I looked at my watch and cleared my throat. "It's one o'clock."

"What?" Marcus was moving toward the door, but he turned to look at me.

"You said forty-eight hours. That's one o'clock the day after tomorrow, not noon."

Several emotions warred for possession of his face: anger, disgust, and a trace of admiration. Disgust won out.

"You won't learn, will you?" He turned and stalked out.

"Nope," I said to an empty shop, "I won't learn."

I had forty-eight hours. Marcus had overestimated by a generous margin the time the inventory would take. With hard work, I could wrap it up this afternoon. That left me with almost two days to find Joan's killer.

And, I thought glumly, maybe end up back in Better Dresses.

# Twelve

Of course, I'd better not cross Greg Marcus's path in the next forty-eight hours. It was a risk, but not a great one. I gathered the lieutenant planned to spend his time trying to pin the killing on Charlie Cornish. I would spend my time otherwise.

I wanted to wrap up the inventory in a hurry, so I went back to the workroom and rummaged around for the records of Joan's purchases. In an old trunk, covered with labels from European hotels, I found a blue cloth binder with the words "Items Bought" scribbled across its cover. I took it to the front room and compared it to my lists.

By sunset I had assigned a value to almost every item in the shop, based on what Joan had originally paid. The exceptions were Edwin; Bruno; five paintings, including the Madonna on Edwin's wall; and the wicked-looking bone-handled knives, the missing one of which was the murder weapon.

The ledger went back only five years, so I returned to the trunk to look for an older one. Under a jumble of office supplies, business cards, old income tax returns, and check stubs, I came across a second notebook that took the purchases back another seven years. On page three, a notation read: "1 stfd dg, prt of lot purch Cncrd Auct Hse fr Bigby—pd to Bigby $17.50."

Decoding it, I decided Bruno must have been one of a group of items that Joan had bought out in Contra Costa County for Austin Bigby, the little red-headed dealer down the street. I smiled, imagining Bigby letting fly with his legendary temper and refusing to allow Bruno in his shop. Joan must have bought the monstrosity from him out of pity for it.

This ledger would probably solve my few remaining problems—a good thing because I was anxious to get out of the shop and on with my murder case. Besides, I was hungry; the chocolate bar had been a long time ago. I decided to take both ledgers and the unidentified paintings with me to compare at home. Edwin and the knives I didn't need; I'd never forget what either looked like. I filled a cardboard carton and loaded it into my car, then went to lock up.

When I came back from checking the rear door, Charlie was standing by the cash register, a bag from a fast-food restaurant in his hand.

"I wanted to apologize," he said, extending it to me. He looked pale and tired but otherwise visibly none the worse from last night's spree.

I burrowed into the bag and pulled out a cheeseburger and Coke. "There's nothing to apologize for. How do you feel?"

"Shitty. Are you done here?"

"Almost." The burger was delicious in my present starved state. "There are a few things I can't place a value on yet. Do you know how much Edwin is worth?"

Charlie shook his head. "Edwin? Quite a lot to Joanie. As

for anybody else, I don't know." He turned and wandered down the aisle toward the mannequin. I followed, carrying my Coke.

"Where did she get him, do you know?"

Charlie shrugged. "He probably came out of some department store that went out of business. Edwin's been here as long as I can remember, ever since I first knew Joanie."

So the ledgers I had in the car wouldn't tell me anything about him. I said, "Van Osten came by this morning. He thinks Edwin was a grandson substitute for Joan. Claims the bit about giving Edwin a picture to look at started about the time the kid died."

Charlie snorted. "That's amateur psychology for you. Joanie was always fond of Edwin, talking to him and the like. The thing about him being an art lover was just a sales gimmick. I remember when Joanie thought of it—it was in the fall, almost a whole year before Chris—that was her grandson—died."

"How do you remember so well?"

His eyes far away, Charlie reached out to straighten the tie of Edwin's sailor suit. "Joanie was always coming to me with outrageous ideas. Some people said she wasn't too much in touch with reality, you know, but she really used her fantasies to her own profit. I mean, she was a successful businesswoman; she owned three quarters of this block." He gestured around us.

"Anyway," he went on, "that fall she came to me all amused about this plan for Edwin's art gallery. We had a good chuckle over it, and then I came over here and helped her pry him up from the floor and move him so he faced the wall, where she was going to hang the pictures."

"Pry him up?"

"Oh, yeah. His shoes were nailed down because he'd fallen over a couple of times, and his face had gotten chipped." He indicated some irregularities on Edwin's nose and left ear. "So I got my hammer and nailed him down again, like he is now."

75

I sighed. "God, she had an imagination, didn't she?"

"She did, and it was catching, you know. She liked to laugh, and I liked to laugh with her. But then Chris died, and Ben Harmon came along. He changed things, kind of...." Charlie's voice drifted off.

"Ben Harmon. The man I met last night." I wanted to leave the way open for Charlie to say more about the bail bondsman.

"Yeah, the bastard. I sent Joanie to him when Chris got busted, and he just started hanging around all the time. He's got a wife and five kids out in the Sunset District, but that didn't stop him. I didn't like him spending time with Joanie. In fact, there're a lot of things I don't like about him, especially the fact he'll profit from the sale of this property."

"How so?"

"That's what he came to tell me last night. Seems Joanie made a verbal agreement to sell out to him. The deal was, Harmon would put up some condominiums with a shopping plaza, and because she swung the sale his way, he'd give Joanie space for her new shop at a reduced rent. Harmon wants us to honor the agreement." Charlie stuck out his lower lip. "I hate to see that son-of-a-bitch get the land, especially with the Ingalls syndicate offering so much more; but if that's what Joanie wanted, that's the way it'll have to be."

"That's too bad, since you could get more money from Ingalls."

Charlie shrugged. "Joanie must have had her reasons." Then he added, "By the way, there's a cop watching the shop."

I went to the window and looked through the deepening dusk at the uniformed officer in the blue-and-white cruiser at the opposite curb. The murderer would never return with that sitting there.

I turned, about to say something to Charlie, but before I could get the words out, an explosion rocked the street. It was a ferocious bang that rattled the windows of the shop.

76

Charlie and I stared at each other in horror, then rushed for the door.

# Thirteen

Charlie and I ran out on the sidewalk. In the next block, flames shot straight up from one of the dilapidated buildings.

"My God!" Charlie shouted. "It's Austin's shop! Come on! He might be in there!" He started running down the street.

The cop at the opposite curb was already on his radio, and seconds later he squealed off toward the fire. I ran back to lock Joan's shop, then remembered I had to lock my car which had her ledgers in it. By the time I got to Austin's, two fire trucks had arrived, and the police were forcing people back, out of danger. Near the front, against the barricade, I saw Charlie and Austin Bigby. So Austin hadn't been inside.

Charlie had his arm around Austin in a protective way. The little red-headed man stood, his long arms hanging down at his sides in a posture of shock. I moved toward them.

As I came up, the two men turned to look at me, Charlie

tightening his hold on Austin, as if I might snatch him away. Tears coursed down Austin's wrinkled face.

"How did it start?" I shouted at Charlie over the roar of water and the crackle of flames.

"Austin says it was like a bomb went off," he yelled back. "He was coming from having a couple of beers, and he saw it. There was that big bang we heard, and then the flames."

The fire raged fiercely, but so far it seemed contained. Austin turned to me, putting a hand on my shoulder. He was so tiny and slumped with despair that he had to reach up.

"Everything's going," he sobbed. "Miss McCone, everything I have, all my stock, it's burning up!"

I hurt for the little shopkeeper, and I took his hand, not knowing what to say.

"Why are these terrible things happening to us?" he wailed. It was as if my touch had opened the floodgates. "What do they want from us anyway? Who *are* they?"

Saying nothing, I squeezed his hand harder. I couldn't take my eyes off the rampaging flames. It was one of the things I feared most: fire out of control.

"Who are They indeed?" I murmured to myself.

There was a hollow roar, then a crash, and sparks flew wildly. I recoiled, stumbling backwards. Charlie let go of Austin, and I grabbed him up, as if he were a child who might be swept away by the crowd. The roof had caved in.

I clung to Austin, breathing hard as I watched the firemen ply their hoses in a desperate attempt to prevent the fire's spread.

"I could have been in there!" Austin screamed hysterically, clutching at me. "I could have burned up in there with all my stuff! They were trying to kill me!"

I ignored his cries and tugged at him, pulling him out of the street onto the sidewalk. Charlie followed, looking helpless. When he didn't reclaim Austin, I tucked the little shopkeeper's arm through mine, trying to calm myself as well. The sidewalks were wet, and I could feel water seeping into my shoes.

"Next time someone *will* be killed!" Austin wept violently.

I didn't know how to comfort him. I thought of saying that his insurance would cover the loss, but I didn't know if he even had insurance, and it wasn't much of a consolation anyway.

"What do they want?" he demanded through his sobs. "Will you tell me what these people want of us?"

"I don't know, Austin. I just don't know." The flames seemed to die down a little, and my breathing felt more normal. "It doesn't make sense to me either."

Austin leaned on me, snuffling. "You were supposed to make some sense of it! We hired you to do that. Joan's dead, and now look what's happened!"

He went off into another fit of sobs. I looked at Charlie, and he spread his hands in a helpless gesture.

"Why couldn't you do anything about it?" Austin demanded, shaking me.

The flames slowly began to subside. "Austin," I said, "you voted against hiring me."

"We voted for you," he protested. "We even paid you. I was treasurer of the Merchants' Association last fall, and I remember writing out the check."

"No, I don't mean then; I mean last night, when you decided not to hire me to investigate Joan's murder." I looked around for Charlie and saw him edge away.

"Last night we did what?" Austin rummaged in his hip pocket and produced a dirty handkerchief. He began to scrub his face and blow his nose. With the flames' subsiding, his hysteria had subsided, too.

"Charlie suggested the Association hire me to look after their interests in the murder investigation. You turned it down." An awful suspicion dawned on me. I started to edge after Charlie.

Austin's swollen face was puzzled. "He never . . . I mean, all we did last night was take a collection for the wreath for Joan's memorial service."

"He didn't say anything about me?"

81

Austin shook his head.

I whirled to look for Charlie and saw him melt into the crowd.

"Damn you, Charlie Cornish," I muttered. Last night he had played games with me, and now he had left me here with little Austin Bigby on my hands. I looked about for someone, anyone, I knew.

My eyes lighted on Dan Efron, the lanky, dark-haired comedian of Salem Street whom everyone called Dandy. I signaled to him, and he came over, seeming for once unlikely to clown around.

"Dan, Austin's awfully upset. Look after him, will you?" I thrust his fellow shopkeeper into his arms before he could protest, then pushed through the crowd in the direction Charlie had gone. The fire had about run its course.

Junk Emporium was locked and, to all appearances, deserted. I went up and pounded on the big front door, knowing I would get no answer if Charlie was hiding inside. After a few minutes, I gave up, kicking the door to emphasize my fury.

My mind staggered under the news of Charlie's deception. What was he hiding? Had he, after all, killed Joan?

I crossed the street to the antique shop. The police guard was nowhere in sight; I supposed he was still at the fire. To make sure the shop was secure, I got out my keys and unlocked the door, flicking the lights on as I stepped in.

The shop looked as if something had exploded there, too. Furniture was tipped at odd angles. Vases lay in jagged shards on the floor. I stared into a smashed mirror and saw a hundred fragments of my own reflection. Even the old pickle crock, van Osten's "distinguished aging receptacle," had tumbled from its shelf, cracking on top of the lid of a child's school desk below.

Only an earthquake or a pair of human hands could have wreaked this havoc. And we hadn't had an earthquake.

I could feel a cool breeze from the workroom. Cautiously I entered it. The flimsy rear door stood partway open, the lock

82

dangling from the splintered frame. So, while everyone, including the police guard, was at the fire, a visitor had come and gone.

I leaned wearily against the workbench, frustration and depression rising simultaneously. The murderer had probably gotten what he wanted this time; the shop had been too thoroughly ransacked for him to have departed empty-handed. I wondered if he had set the fire to cause a distraction. It seemed extreme, but the murder had been extreme, too. Something very important must be at stake.

"What?" I muttered. "What the hell did he get?"

I rummaged through a drawer under the workbench where I'd seen a padlock earlier that day and secured the back door with it. Then I quickly checked through the ravaged shop to see if I could tell what was missing. None of the objects that I remembered inventorying were gone, although many had been totally destroyed. I stopped in front of Edwin, who stood unharmed in his iron shoes.

"You're lucky, buddy," I told him. "At least your feet are nailed to the floor." I had developed a strange kinship with the cherubic little mannequin. Perhaps he reminded me of my brothers at their first communion.

I knew I should call the police and report the break-in, but that would involve a lot of time and tiresome questions. Besides, the police guard would return and discover it soon enough. I could go through my inventory sheets now and maybe figure out what was missing, but that could last all night, and the object itself might not necessarily help me identify the killer.

There must be a shortcut to that information, I told myself, and I might stumble on it if I followed the course I'd been planning before the fire. Ben Harmon's name had been cropping up over and over, and I was very anxious to talk with the bail bondsman.

# *Fourteen*

The sign was on Bryant Street, in the seedy district near the Hall of Justice. Harmon's storefront was well lit tonight, a neon oasis in the darkness around Seventh Street. I parked directly in front, unwilling to travel those unfriendly sidewalks any further than necessary.

The reception room was tiny and crammed with battered plastic furniture. A slender, dark-haired young man stood beside the desk. He wore a black suit with a slick sheen to its fabric and smoked a small, thin cigar. He looked at me, curling his lip.

"Can I help you?" He spoke with a thick Spanish accent.

I gave him my card and asked if Harmon was in.

He looked at the card, raising a scornful eyebrow, and left the room without a word. I wondered if he treated everyone who came in like that. If so, Harmon was sure to lose business to the other bondsmen in the district. On the other hand, if you were there in the first place, maybe you were expecting to be treated that way.

I didn't have to wait long for Harmon. About two minutes later, he emerged from a narrow hallway to the left. He was wearing another flashy suit, blue plaid this time, and looked as fresh as if it were morning. Although he extended his carefully tended hand to me in a pleasant manner, Harmon's eyes flickered with annoyance.

"Miss McCone, what can I do for you?"

"I'm cooperating with the police on the Albritton killing," I lied, "and I want to ask you a few questions that have occurred to me since we spoke last night."

"This is a strange time to call with questions." He checked his watch.

"It's a strange time for someone to be at work."

"Not in my business."

I smiled. "Nor in mine. I often go about interviewing people at night."

Harmon gave a resigned sigh. "Well, let's go back to my office then." The neon light bounced off his thick glasses as he waved me toward the hallway.

I started along, then hesitated as the dark young man emerged from a door to the right. He nodded gravely and motioned me on. As I went, I glanced at the framed newspaper clippings that lined the walls. They were about clients, guilty and not guilty. Apparently Harmon was proud of anyone who paid his stiff fees, avarice being as impartial as justice, I supposed.

Harmon and I entered the room at the end of the hall, the Latin type following us. He closed the door and took up a position against the wall, like a sentry. I could smell the sickly odor of too much after shave under the cigar smoke.

I looked questioningly at Harmon.

"Don't mind Frankie," he said. "He's my bodyguard. Goes everywhere with me and does everything I tell him to."

I got his all-too-obvious point.

The office where we stood was deeply carpeted and paneled but with sleazy materials, as if Harmon didn't expect to occupy it long. The bail bondsman gestured toward a naugahyde armchair, and I took a seat.

"Would you like a drink, Miss McCone? I can offer you something better than Charlie's cheap gin tonight."

"As a matter of fact, I could use a drink."

"Bourbon?"

"Fine."

Harmon went to a small wooden keg that protruded from the wall at shoulder height, opened its hinged front, and produced all the fixings for a cocktail party.

"Handy little gadget, isn't it?" he said, all affability now as he measured liquor into two glasses. "Looks just like a wall decoration until you open it. At any rate, it has my wife fooled."

I couldn't imagine Harmon shrinking from a wife's disapproval. I took the glass from his outstretched hand and watched him sit down behind the broad expanse of desk.

"Speaking of drinking," he said, "how is our friend Cornish doing?"

"He seems fully recovered. The last time I saw him was at a fire over on Salem Street half an hour ago. Austin Bigby's shop burned down."

Harmon sipped at his bourbon, raising an eyebrow. "Arson?"

"Possibly. There was some sort of explosion. It looks like a total loss."

"Poor Bigby. They've had their troubles over there." Harmon looked genuinely surprised, even puzzled. "First the vandalisms, then Joan's death. Charlie will never get over that."

"I thought their relationship had cooled off. Charlie seemed to regard you as a rival."

"Charlie." He sighed. "Joan and I were just casual friends, and he knows it. I really can't figure what Joan saw in him, but I doubt anyone could have taken Charlie's place in her affections. She had a weakness for lost souls, and more or less took him under her wing when he appeared on Salem Street. That would be over twenty years ago, right after Joan divorced her husband."

"Where did Charlie come from anyway?" In light of his deception about asking the Merchants' Association to hire me, I wanted to take a good close look at the big junkman.

"Who knows?" Harmon spread his hands in an empty gesture. "He got into the business as a scavenger, one of those people who run around at night raiding garbage cans."

I was familiar with the scavengers. A couple of them were active in my neighborhood, and I often woke late at night to the rumbling of their carts in the alley.

"That's kind of an unsavory start," I commented.

Harmon nodded. "Charlie was addicted to junk, you might say. When his room filled up with the stuff he'd scavenged, he rented the store on Salem Street and sold it all. I don't think he ever expected to make money off it, but pretty soon he was able to buy his building and the street became his permanent home."

And where did he get the money to rent the store in the first place? I wondered. Aloud I said, "But, much as he interests me, I didn't come here to talk about Charlie. Right now I want to know when you finalized your agreement with Joan to buy the Salem Street properties and put up condominiums."

Harmon started. "Where did you hear about that?"

"Around the street. How long before her death did you make the agreement?"

He regarded me warily. "Not that it's any of your business, but we agreed on it over a month ago—long before she died."

"And, as part of that agreement, you were to provide her with space for her new shop at a reduced rent?"

He scowled. "You seem to have all the details. Joan couldn't afford to move to a new place otherwise."

I thought of Hank's description of the Albritton estate: substantial. "For how long?"

"What do you mean?"

"How long would the reduced rent have gone on?"

"Oh." He waved his hand vaguely. "Until she got on her feet again."

I watched him for a few seconds, then asked, "Is there any reason, if she were pressed for money, that she would have sold to you when she could have gotten a much higher price from the Ingalls syndicate?"

"Who told you that?"

"I saw Mrs. Ingalls yesterday." To myself I added, From a distance.

Harmon paused, looking down into his glass. Behind me, the bodyguard shifted against the wall.

"Well," Harmon finally said with a forced leer, "you have to remember Joan and I were extremely good friends."

Hank had been right about Harmon: he wasn't very smart. "A few minutes ago you said you and Joan were just casual friends. Which was it?"

Anger flickered in his eyes as he realized he'd contradicted himself. "I don't go around broadcasting my affairs!" he snapped. "I'm a married man!"

Stifling a smile, I nodded gravely. "I understand."

"Besides," Harmon added, "Joan wasn't a very good businesswoman. She wasn't too . . . too stable, you know."

Then how did she amass such a sizable estate? I asked myself. "I've heard that from other people. Oliver van Osten mentioned her habit of talking to that mannequin she called Edwin. He took her routine about Edwin's art gallery as evidence her mind had been affected by her grandson's death."

"Van Osten said she was crazy?"

"That was the general idea."

"Well, for Christ's sake." Harmon fell silent, picking at his well-manicured nails.

"How well do you know van Osten?"

He looked up, his eyes confused. "Van Osten? Not well. I mean, I've heard of him is all. What the hell are you driving at?"

"I'm not driving at anything, Mr. Harmon. I'm just collecting information that will help me find Joan's killer."

"What makes you think I have any?"

"I have my reasons."

Behind me, there was a quick movement. I turned my head. The Spanish bodyguard's dark face was only inches from mine. His breath smelled bad and his bright black eyes glinted with hostility.

"Frankie, relax," Harmon's voice said. To me he added, "Frankie doesn't like me upset."

He's seen too many gangster movies on the late show, I decided. I took my cue. "Why are you upset?"

"I don't like being badgered by little girls playing detective." He stood up.

Harmon was hiding something from me, and not very skillfully either. I took what seemed like a big risk and remained sitting. "I'm not playing, Mr. Harmon. This is for real. What were you doing over at Bigby's shop tonight?"

"I wasn't anywhere near Bigby's shop!"

"Or at Albritton's the night she was murdered?"

Behind me, the bodyguard hissed furiously. It would have been laughable if I weren't so frightened.

"What are you talking about?" Harmon demanded. "I hadn't seen her in days!"

"Then you won't mind telling me where you were at the time she was killed."

"I don't have to tell you anything."

Of course he didn't. I hadn't expected him to. But his behavior had told me a great deal.

Harmon's face was florid to the top of his bald head. He came around the desk toward me. I felt the bodyguard pressing against the back of my chair.

"Listen, you nosy little bitch," Harmon said in a low shaking voice, his hands balled into fists. "I'm not taking any more crap off of you!"

I kept my voice from revealing my fear and asked, "Are you going to call the police names when they come here with the same questions?"

He stopped short in front of me, his voice growling deep in his throat. "You little fool! Do you think I swallowed that line about you cooperating with the police? Greg Marcus told me he was only humoring you. When he hears about this, you'll be lucky you don't end up in jail!"

I was certain Harmon had swallowed my line initially or he never would have talked to me, but his mention of Marcus threw me off. I wondered what their connection was. Could Marcus be a crooked cop?

Harmon made a savage motion to Frankie. "Get her out of here." He turned away, toward his desk.

The young man yanked me from the chair by my arm. He walked me through the door and down the hallway, his fingers biting into my flesh. I didn't resist: preservation lay in going quietly.

At the front door, Frankie kept his grip on my arm, mashing my body between his own and the door frame. The combined odors of his breath and his loathsome after shave were overpowering, and I tried to squeeze away through the door. For an instant, I wondered if he could have been the intruder I'd struggled with in the shop the night before. No, I decided, he was much too slender and odorous.

"I will make a warning to you, Miss McCone," Frankie said, his nostrils flaring in distaste. "When a young lady asks bold questions, many bad things can happen to her. You do not wish this. ¿Comprende?" He looked as if he might spit in my face.

I pushed him away and wrenched my arm from his grip. "Gracias, Frankie. Comprendo."

I backed through the swinging door and across the sidewalk toward my car, fighting down nausea. Frankie's threat hadn't particularly bothered me, but the touch of his body literally made me sick. It was important I remain here, though, waiting for Harmon's next move. I was surprised at how much our conversation had thrown the bail bondsman off, and it was possible he might panic and do something revealing. If he did, I wanted to be on hand for it.

# Fifteen

I moved my car down to the corner, where I could see both the front of Harmon's place and the exit from the one-way alley behind it. If he decided to leave either way, I would have him covered.

About ten minutes later, Harmon came out onto Bryant Street, wearing a raincoat. He paused, looking around, then went to the curb and unlocked the door of a gold Lincoln Continental.

I slumped lower in my seat, watching him in the side-view mirror. When he had pulled out of his parking space and gone past me, I started up and followed.

Harmon led me out Geary Street into the Avenues. I recalled Charlie's remark about the bail bondsman's palace in the Sunset District. Possibly Harmon was going home to bed.

The Lincoln was easy to follow, and traffic wasn't heavy. I stayed two lanes over, a few car-lengths back. We continued out Geary, past Park Presidio, the numbers of the Avenues getting higher. I knew now that Harmon wasn't heading home because he hadn't crossed the park.

At Forty-third Avenue, the road made a little "Y," the right half becoming Point Lobos Avenue. The Lincoln went that way, toward the sea. I followed, slowing in the middle of a block when it turned into the last street before the large parking area overlooking the water. Through the thick fog that enveloped everything, I saw the brake lights of the other car as it stopped at the curb.

Harmon's tall figure emerged from the car and approached a three-story rough-shingled building on the corner. I timed myself three minutes, then got out of my car and went down the sidewalk. The fog swirled damply around me, providing good cover. I could hardly see the houses that lined the street, and I had an unreal feeling I might step off the edge of the world at any minute.

The modern building resembled two shoe boxes standing on end. The bottom apartments had fenced-in patios, and the balconies of the second and third floors were isolated from each other, designed for maximum privacy. Tonight, all the windows were dark save for a dim light behind draperies on the top floor.

Another light shone on the mailboxes in the shrubbery-filled entryway. I went up and examined them. There were six, each with a little buzzer next to it. The metal mouth of an intercom smiled up at me. Five mailboxes had names on them that I didn't recognize, but the sixth name interested me very much.

Oliver van Osten.

The fake-antique dealer whom Harmon had said he didn't know.

Van Osten's apartment number was five, and from what I could guess of the layout, it would be the third-floor one with the light on. I retreated from the building, thankful I was wearing black, and crossed to a large wooded area between the street and the parking lot. From there I could watch the apartment unobserved.

The fog dimmed my view of the window, making it a

luminous screen on which no film played. I stood in the clammy underbrush, shivering and wishing for a heavier jacket.

A minute or so passed, and then a stocky figure appeared, silhouetted on the drapes. Van Osten. Or was it? I had seen that figure before.

It went away, then reappeared, pacing.

A second figure joined it, a tall, slightly stoop-shouldered one. Ben Harmon was about that height, and his shoulders rounded a little, too. It waved its arms in an agitated gesture, then went away. The stocky shape followed.

"Incredible!" I whispered aloud. No wonder the stocky figure looked familiar. The last time I had seen it in silhouette, though, it had been running, not pacing. Running along Salem Street, away from the havoc it had wreaked on Charlie's shop. I was sure I was right.

Still, I couldn't see van Osten as the original vandal; it just didn't fit. But if not, why was he now running around hurling bricks at Charlie's windows? He had to want something from Joan's shop very badly—enough, maybe, to justify setting Austin's entire building on fire earlier tonight.

I leaned forward, watching the little shadow play across the street. I was so absorbed in it, in fact, that I didn't turn fast enough when I heard twigs snap in the brush behind me.

The arm that hooked around my neck was lean, but very strong. I sagged backwards against a wiry body, my scream choked off at its source. I was immediately aware of the smell of too much after shave and cigar smoke.

Hot breath tickled the hair over my ear, and the heavily accented voice of Harmon's Spanish thug said mockingly, "So, the little detective does not heed my warning. You think you are so clever, driving right along behind Mr. Harmon, but I am driving right along behind you."

I struggled, but he tightened his grip.

"¡Pobrecita!" Frankie chuckled. "You must not fight so hard. It is of no use. Now we will go to Mr. Harmon and Mr. van Osten, and you will see what happens to people who interfere." He dragged me toward the street.

I put down my terror and thought of the moves I'd

95

practiced in self-defense classes. I dug my heels into the ground and created as much resistance as I could. I had to stop him before he dragged me into that building.

Just before we got to the curb, my attacker stopped, breathing hard. He wasn't a big man, and I was enough burden to tire him. The pause gave my reflexes time to wake up. I shot my right leg back around his, then rolled my hips and pitched forward with all my strength. He toppled, flipping and hitting the ground on his back, grunting heavily.

Shocked that it had actually worked, I stared down at him. Then I dashed back into the underbrush, stumbling and slipping on the wet ground. I heard him gasp. I hadn't disabled him for long.

I ran wildly through the bushes and trees, falling and sliding down toward the parking lot. Footsteps scrambled fast behind me.

Several cars were parked at the edge of the lot, fog thick about them. Foghorns bellowed as I raced through the lot to the walk beside the Great Highway. Footsteps crunched back on the gravel.

I ran blindly down the sidewalk, knowing Cliff House, the restaurant that overlooked the sea, was not far ahead. The footsteps now slapped along on the pavement after me and seemed to be gaining.

Out of the heavy mist, a couple of dark shapes appeared. I couldn't swerve, and I plowed into them, crying out in shock.

"Hey, what the hell are you doing?" an angry male voice demanded.

I whirled and careened down the sidewalk.

"Hey, damn it!" the voice shouted a few seconds later. "Once was enough!"

Evidently my pursuer had followed the same collision course.

The lights of Cliff House were before me now. I raced toward them, avoiding strollers, and burst through the door of the restaurant, breathing hard. I wasn't sure if Frankie would come in after me or not.

Ahead I saw the stairs to the dining room and the upper bar. I wanted to find shelter in the ladies' room, but its downstairs location would be a trap. I climbed slowly, my knees weak. The bar was crowded and brightly lit, a cheerful haven from the dismal, foggy sea beyond huge windows. It would also be a haven from my attacker. I stood in the doorway, looking for a place to sit.

A group of people in Levis and windbreakers occupied a table in the far window bay. As I stood there, one of them, a woman with a round, freckled face and dark hair, spied me. She waved, her face crinkling into a wide grin.

"Hey, Sharon! Hello! Come on over!"

It was my friend Paula Mercer, a fine arts graduate from Berkeley who worked for the de Young Museum.

Almost collapsing with relief, I started across the bar. The group rearranged themselves as Paula greeted me, introducing everyone by first names and adding asides that led me to believe they were part of the local arts and crafts crowd. As I sat down and one of the guys called for another glass of wine, I glanced at the entryway.

Frankie stood there, his shiny suit rumpled and sweat-stained, his tie askew. His eyes scanned the room and came to rest on me. Our glances locked, and an icy dread frosted my limbs.

"Sharon?" Paula's voice was concerned. "What's the matter?"

I dragged my eyes away from Frankie. "What?"

"I said, what's wrong? You just turned a ghastly shade of pale!"

The waitress placed a glass of Chablis in front of me, and I grabbed it, gulping deeply. "I'll be all right," I said. "I'm just in a little trouble."

Comprehension flooded Paula's features. "I thought you looked strange when you came in. Is it a case?"

I nodded. "I don't know what I would have done if you hadn't been here. Will you help me?"

"Of course."

"Don't leave me, that's all. Not for a second. And when

97

you go, give me a ride to my car. It's parked up on Point Lobos."

Paula frowned. "Don't worry about a thing. But shouldn't you tell the police if someone's out to get you?"

I glanced at the entryway. Frankie had disappeared.

"No, it's not that sort of thing," I said. "Don't you worry either." I felt slightly more normal, thanks to the wine.

"Look, Paula," I went on, realizing my friend could help with one of my more mundane problems, "I don't want to go into it now, but the case I'm on involves taking an inventory of some art objects."

"You?" Paula clapped a hand to her forehead. "God help whomever the inventory's for!"

I smiled. Paula's joking and the chatter of the group around us was doing a lot to restore my sense of reality. "Anyway, there are some paintings, probably done by local artists, that I can't fix a value on. If I dragged them over to the de Young tomorrow, do you think you could take a look at them?"

She nodded. "I've got a big exhibit to put together, but I should be done around two. Why don't you stop by then?"

I said I would, and we turned our attention to the rest of the group. It was after one in the morning when we left, a large, somewhat drunken crowd that provided perfect cover for me. Paula drove me to my car in her van, waiting while I checked the MG over to make sure Frankie hadn't disabled it. It surprised me, but the car was okay. Still, I was expecting some kind of trouble and circled the block several times when I got home, watching for suspicious figures. I parked as close as I could and rushed in, clutching the carton containing the paintings and Joan's records. The apartment seemed okay, too; for whatever reasons, Frankie had, I hoped, given up for the night.

Tired and shaken as I was, I sat down cross-legged on my bed to check with my answering service.

"It's been a busy night," Claudia, the operator, told me. "Hank Zahn called at ten and again at eleven. No message either time. Your mother called from San Diego and com-

98

plained about you not being home, like she always does. That was at ten fifteen. A Mrs. Cara Ingalls called twice, asked that you call her tomorrow at her office. And then a Gregory Marcus called at ten twenty-three, left a number. Said it was important. Revised the number at eleven and called again at twelve fifteen, talking as if he suspected me of not giving you your messages." Claudia's professional pride was wounded.

"Don't let him bother you," I told her. Claudia, like the companionship and wine at Cliff House, was helping me pull myself together.

"What's with him anyway? He sounds mean and sexy." Claudia, a friend who gave me cut rates on the expensive twenty-four-hour service, loved to speculate about the callers, and we'd had many interesting conversations in the dead of night.

"Mean he is, but forget the sexy," I said, yawning. "Do me a favor, will you?" Ben Harmon's mention of Marcus had made me wary.

"Sure."

"If Marcus calls again, tell him you haven't talked to me." I didn't like to ask people to lie for me, but Claudia had long ago explained her operator's code of ethics. It was very complicated, involving concepts of client confidentiality that would astonish even the legal-minded Hank.

"Right. What about your mother?"

"I'll try to get her tomorrow. Probably one of my brothers has gotten busted again, or one of my sisters is having another baby. No big deal." I got the number Cara Ingalls had left with Claudia, then said good-night and hung up.

Cara Ingalls: I had temporarily forgotten her, but the message on my card had interested her enough to make her try to reach me twice. Talking with her could well add many missing pieces to my puzzle—or change the shape of it altogether.

And Charlie Cornish: tomorrow I'd have to wring his story out of him. He might throw some light on the van Osten–Harmon connection.

I undressed sitting on the bed, then snuggled down under the heavy quilt. A residue of the terror I'd felt while running through the fog still clung to me, warring with my exhaustion. In minutes, exhaustion won out.

# Sixteen

At eight the next morning, I could tell it was going to be a beautiful day. A pre-dawn rainstorm had washed the air clean, and early sunshine brought the kids out into my alley, rioting up and down on their skateboards before school.

I watched them, thankful I was in any condition to enjoy the morning. Then, banishing my morbid reflections, I sat down on my bed with a cup of coffee and Joan's records. I wanted to wrap up the inventory before I called Cara Ingalls.

Hank was right about Albritton: for a successful businesswoman, she had kept remarkably slapdash records. Within an hour, though, I had found a value for the set of bone-handled knives. Edwin I evaluated at a flat hundred dollars, most of it sentiment. The five paintings—two still lifes, the Madonna, a seascape, and a city scene—remained questions that Paula Mercer would hopefully answer when we met that afternoon.

Assuming she would, I had only two loose ends, both shipments Joan had apparently ordered, prepaid, from van Osten. The final two ledger entries indicated one that hadn't arrived as far as I could tell, due last Monday; the other was slated to appear tomorrow, Friday. I wrote the order numbers in my notebook. If Hank thought it important, he could query van Osten. Of course, by that time van Osten might be in custody for vandalism . . . or worse. It all depended on the outcome of my activities today.

At nine o'clock, I dialed Cara Ingalls's number. The switchboard put me through to a secretary, who took my name and left me on hold. Five minutes later, the husky voice from the cocktail party came on the line. I suggested we meet sometime today.

"Today? Sorry, no. I'm booked up, right through nine this evening."

"You must have fifteen minutes. I can be there in half an hour."

"Can't we discuss it on the phone?"

"I'm not sure you'd want to."

She paused. Then, "I planned to have lunch at my desk today, but I guess I can get away. Can you meet me at one o'clock?"

I said I could, and she named a restaurant on Battery Street.

"I'll be outside," she said. "How will I know you?"

"Don't worry. I'll recognize you." I hung up quickly.

I had plenty of time to spare, so I dressed, tidied the apartment, and took out the garbage. At the big bin downstairs, I ran into Tim O'Riley, the building manager. Tim was a paunchy Irishman who drank beer from the time he got up until he passed out in mid-afternoon.

"You're here," Tim commented in surprise as I dumped my garbage.

"Yeah. Why didn't you think I was?"

"You weren't answering your door." A crafty look came over Tim's puffy face. "Oh, I get it. You're avoiding him."

I couldn't remember anybody coming to my door. I turned to face Tim. "Avoiding who?"

"The Mexican guy who was at your door a few minutes ago."

"What did he look like?" The words came out sharp, and Tim stared at me.

"Like a Mexican. Little. Dark. Skinny. Smoked a cigar. Walked like his back hurt him."

In spite of his alcoholic haze, Tim was a good observer. Of course, there were a lot of Chicanos in the neighborhood. It could have been someone selling life insurance. But then, I had flipped Frankie on his back last night.

"Did you talk to him?"

"I sure did. At first I thought he was trying to look through the glass in the door. You know how people will. So I asked him what he wanted, and he said he guessed you wasn't home. Then I came down here a while later and found him sneaking around in the alley, looking up at your windows. I told him to get, and he got."

I was certain it had been Frankie, and I didn't like him on my home territory, not one bit. "Thanks for sending him away, Tim. Let me know if you see him again, will you?"

"No trouble," Tim said. "I guess in your business you gotta expect creeps hanging around." He picked up his beer can and shuffled inside.

Frankie couldn't harm me in my own building in broad daylight, I thought. Still, I went upstairs and got my .38 Special from the locked box where I kept it. I loaded it and put it in an inner compartment of my bag, where it was easy to reach. Then I sat down and called my friend Bob at the San Francisco bureau of the *Wall Street Journal*.

Bob sounded stuffy and proper when he came on the line, befitting a writer for that stately publication, but when I identified myself he dropped the pretense. Unknown to the *Journal*, Bob wrote lurid true-crime stories on the side, and I'd met him a few years before while he was researching one, a case I'd been peripherally involved in.

103

"What can you tell me about a Mrs. Cara Ingalls, real-estate person?" I asked him.

"She makes a lot of money and is crazy about weird hats," he said. "Seriously, do you want me to look up her biography?"

"If you don't mind."

Bob returned to the phone a few minutes later. "This is pretty sketchy, and I don't know the lady myself, but it's all we have: born, San Jose. Thirty-six years old. Three years San Jose State, majoring in architecture. Put herself through school selling houses—that was in the days of the big boom down there—but quit to join her firm's commercial division in San Francisco before she got her degree. List of various honors received and memberships—I won't go into that. Formed her own firm, Ingalls and Associates, three years ago. They hold many of the options on the land in Yerba Buena. Offhand, I'd say she invested her commissions well."

"Is that it?"

"Just about. There's not much on her personal life, which is what I assume you're after. One marriage to Douglas Ingalls, local socialite. No children. Divorced Ingalls four years ago. From what I know of Ingalls, that was a good move. All he does is drink and sail his boat on the Bay. Anyway, Mrs. Ingalls lives in a condominium on Nob Hill, has a summer home at Tahoe, and is a generous supporter of the arts. That's all we have."

I thanked Bob; before hanging up, he reminded me to get in touch if I ran across any good murders.

The sidewalks of the financial district teemed with lunchtime strollers. Shifting packs of what appeared to be young executives roved about, enjoying the sunshine and eying the girls who ate bag lunches in the outdoor plazas. The normally gray canyon of Montgomery Street was bathed in light, and smartly dressed office workers moved lazily across its intersections. I was sure a lot of people would be back at their desks very late today.

As I approached our meeting place, I spied the imposing

figure of Cara Ingalls on the sidewalk. I glanced at my watch and smiled. I had definitely interested her: she was five minutes early.

I crossed the street, admiring Ingalls's cashmere coat-dress that met brown leather boots at mid-calf. Bob had been right about Ingalls's fondness for millinery: today she wore a little wine-colored felt job tilted rakishly over one eye. She made me, in my simple pants and corduroy jacket, feel like a mere slip of a girl.

I approached Ingalls, identifying myself, and she gave me a glance that said I looked the way I felt. "We'd better hurry; they're holding a table," she said, ushering me inside the restaurant.

Ingalls commanded excellent service. Within minutes, a bevy of waiters had installed us in a corner booth and taken our orders. The restaurant boasted Italian specialties, so I ordered cannelloni and white wine. Ingalls must have been on a diet, since she chose grapefruit juice and shrimp salad without dressing. I had never had to worry about excess weight in my life; as I munched on a piece of sourdough bread, I felt I was getting back at her for making me feel young and inelegant.

We had a pretty boring chat about the weather until our lunches came; then I said, "Let's talk about the Salem Street properties now. Does your offer still stand?"

Ingalls nodded. "I spoke with Mr. Cornish this morning. He's assuming responsibility for the decision, although the probate of Mrs. Albritton's estate will naturally slow the proceedings."

So Charlie was keeping her on the hook. That indicated he might not honor Harmon's claim on the land.

I asked, "What have you heard about counter-offers?"

She shrugged. "My sources say my offer is far and away the highest. I want that land, and I'm prepared to go as high as necessary."

"What's so desirable about Salem Street?"

"Location," she answered promptly. "Proximity to the Civic Center. People working there are a ready market for condominiums, to say nothing of shops and restaurants. There's no end to the potential."

"I'm sure other people have thought of that."

"Of course. But I have the resources to do it."

I was beginning to enjoy talking with Cara Ingalls. She was my kind of woman, one who made her way on her own steam and refused to be held back. That was what I had always done, although without anything near her financial success.

I said, "Your sources, who do they say you're competing against?"

She smiled. "Only one organization, that Western Addition Credit Union."

So Harmon's offer was not common knowledge. "You seem pleased."

"I am. They can hardly match my offer. It's a good thing, too: this city doesn't need another shoddy low-income housing project cluttering up the landscape."

I had seen the credit union's plans the previous fall, and they hadn't looked so shoddy to me. "I hear it's quite well designed. And the city certainly does need more reasonably priced housing." I thought of the huge rent I paid for my old-fashioned studio.

Ingalls laughed shortly. "Come on. Look at the trash that moves into those places. Each family with dozens of unruly kids writing on the walls—if they can write at all—and dirtying the place up. Those people shouldn't be allowed to live here."

Her tone was matter-of-fact, and it shocked me. "Where do you suggest they go?"

"Anywhere, just so I don't have to look at their mess."

"That's a rather calloused attitude."

Her eyes narrowed. They were a strange, pure amber color, reinforcing my impression of her catlike quality. "Miss McCone, let's have none of your girlish liberal sentiments. The world is a big, harsh place. I'm surprised in your profession . . ."

"I try to hang on to my ideals. Granted, it's hard . . ."

106

Ingalls laughed bitterly. The laugh struck me as a little off-key.

"Let me tell you a story about ideals," she said in a low voice, leaning forward toward me. "I was the youngest in my family, the only girl. My father was an architect, and we were all brought up to be professional people. My three brothers were to be an attorney, a doctor, and a dentist, in that order. I was to follow in my father's footsteps as an architect—so I thought."

Her yellow eyes held mine. I wondered why she was telling me this, but I didn't want to interrupt.

"My father died when I was sixteen. Of a heart attack on the golf course. My closest brother had completed dental school two months before. After the funeral, my mother and I found out my father had canceled his life insurance the day of my brother's graduation. His boys were educated, so there was no need for it any more; my mother and I didn't count."

The story chilled me. "So you put yourself through school."

"Not all the way." She shook her head, her mouth twisted. "For three years I did. I worked nights, studied while I sat in empty houses on weekends, waiting to show them. Then one day I woke up and said, 'What in hell am I doing busting my ass to become some sort of living monument to my old man, the son-of-a-bitch who thought me less than human?' So I quit studying architecture and went full time into real estate. I made it big: I've already cleared more money than my old man made in his entire life. I only wish the old bastard could know!"

I closed my eyes against Cara Ingalls's seething psyche. For some reason she was trying to transfer the weight of her emotions to me, a burden I in no way could handle right now.

I said, "But we're getting off the subject. There are a few more things I want to ask about your offer for the Salem Street property."

Ingalls looked down at her salad and began rooting through it with her fork, as if she might find something there amid the shrimps and bibb lettuce to soothe her unhealed wound. When she looked up, her eyes were calm again, with a shadow of tired defeat. "And they are?"

"Did you meet with Joan Albritton again after that time you bought the painting from her?"

Her eyes widened. "What painting?"

"You came to her shop last October and bought an inexpensive painting. I thought you were checking her out."

"*You* thought?" She set her fork down carefully.

"Yes. I was in the shop that day, talking to Joan."

"I see." The yellow eyes moved rapidly, calculating. "No, I never did see her again. The money was well spent though, even if the picture did go in the garbage. I wanted to see who I was dealing with before I made an offer. I was able to go in quite a bit lower than I would have, had I not seen how . . . foolish and eccentric Joan Albritton was."

Any sympathy I'd felt for Cara Ingalls vanished with her careless assessment of the little antique dealer. In its place, suspicion rose: Why had Ingalls thought the climate was right for an offer? Her visit to the shop had been weeks before the notice condemning the buildings, when the Salem Street people had been militantly opposed to any real-estate deal.

I asked a few additional questions, hoping to make Ingalls contradict herself, but she replied in technicalities. I gained some insight into the workings of her profession but very little information on the bidding for the Salem Street properties. Our lunches finished, I insisted on paying the tab and said good-bye to her on the sidewalk in front of the restaurant.

It was a shame about Cara Ingalls, I thought, as I started down the sidewalk to the place I'd left my car. She was an intelligent, strong woman, and strikingly attractive, but in spite of that I couldn't help pitying her. In her rush to make it, she had left a part of her humanity behind, and her desperate reaching out to me signaled that she felt its loss.

Well, that was her problem. Right now mine seemed more pressing. It was time for my appointment with Paula at the de Young, and I had to go home to pick up the paintings I wanted to show her. I was hoping Frankie wouldn't be waiting there for me.

# Seventeen

When I asked for Paula Mercer, the man collecting admissions at the de Young gestured toward the center of the museum and didn't charge me the seventy-five-cent fee. I walked across the pillared entryway to the big central area. Toward the end, I saw a huge tapestry hanging on cords from the high skylit ceiling.

Paula suddenly appeared around the edge of the tapestry, waving at me, her mouth full of pins. She wore faded jeans and a green sweater, and had her dark hair hitched up in two horsetails on either side of her head.

She spat the pins into her hand as I approached, her pretty round face breaking into a wide smile of greeting.

"Sharon, I've absolutely got to get the backing on this thing before I can take any time off." Paula was one of the people who set up the museum's special exhibits.

I looked up at the tapestry, which hung twelve feet or more in the air. Its top edge was clamped to a long pole by

111

several of what looked like trouser hangers. "It's awfully big. How do you manage?"

"Not easily. Why don't you wander around for a while? Then we can go get some tea."

"Fine. I haven't been to a museum in years."

Paula stuck the pins back in her mouth and began climbing up a tall work platform behind the tapestry. I hoped she wouldn't swallow any of them.

I kept on toward the back of the museum. A tour was assembled there, and the paintings didn't appeal to me, so I turned into the maze of little galleries to one side, stopping here and there when something caught my fancy. The rooms were chill and quiet, and the air conditioning hummed faintly. I relaxed, enjoying the silence.

As I turned into one of the last galleries in that wing, I stopped abruptly on the threshold, surprised by a familiar figure seated on a bench in the center of the room. I started to back out the door when Greg Marcus looked up and saw me.

There were weary lines on his face, and his shoulders slumped a little. Only a trace of sarcasm showed in the smile he gave me.

"Now who's following whom?"

There was no way to go but into the room. "It looks that way, doesn't it? Actually, I'm here to see a friend on the staff, but she's tied up right now. You come here often?" Remembering our last meeting, I felt uncomfortable, a feeling compounded by the surprise of running across the lieutenant in a museum, the last place I'd have expected to find him.

"Occasionally." Marcus patted the bench next to him and I sat, reluctantly. "This is as good a place to wait for your friend as any," he said. "We're in good company, you know. Those three portraits are Rembrandts."

I hesitated, not wanting to reveal my ignorance of art. It would only give him something else to needle me with. Also, I felt I was intruding on something private. I shifted uncomfortably on the bench, not wanting to be there, but not

112

knowing how to get up and leave. Marcus turned to me with a slight smile.

"You're wondering why I'm not out solving that murder?"

I shrugged. "You can't work all the time."

"No, you can't, but there are days when I think I should, and this is one of them. When things really start getting me down, I come over here."

I wondered what had happened in the last twenty-four hours to make him speak so openly to me. "Doing that," I asked, "helps?"

"Sure. Someone once taught me about the tranquilizing effect of sitting like this in a museum, holding still and really *seeing* the paintings. So I come here, and it works. And afterwards I can think more clearly." He gave me a swift glance, trying to see if I understood.

I wondered if the friend in question had been a woman. When he didn't go on, I said, "Beats Valium."

He laughed, and we sat in silence for a minute or two. I wasn't getting too much out of the Rembrandts, but I was really seeing the lieutenant for the first time. I was pleasantly surprised by Marcus's sensitivity, and I wanted very much to believe him an honest cop, but Harmon's mention of him still called up my distrust. I didn't know how deep his relationship with the bail bondsman went.

Cautiously I said, "I was talking with Ben Harmon, the bail bondsman, last night. He said you told him you were just humoring Hank Zahn and me by letting us in on the Albritton investigation."

"Harmon?" Marcus looked surprised. "He's a rough character. How well do you know him?"

"Not well." I waited, hoping he would say something to lay my suspicions to rest.

"Our friend Harmon seems to be popping up all over the place," he commented.

"What do you mean?"

"Remember yesterday—I'm sure you do—when you got so angry because you thought I had had you followed?"

I nodded.

113

"I mentioned I had my sources. Well, in this case, the source was Harmon. I ran into him over at the Hall of Justice that morning, and he said he'd met you at Cornish's. He tried to pump me about your involvement in the case. That was when I said I was humoring you. I didn't know what his interest was, but I don't trust the man."

"I see." Marcus was either honest or an excellent liar. I decided to go with honesty. "Actually, it's just as well I ran into you, because I have some developments to report." I went on to tell him of the ransacked shop, Harmon's offer for the Salem Street properties, his late-night visit to van Osten, and my frantic flight to Cliff House. He listened, a frown etching a deep line between his dark eyebrows.

"This is all very interesting," he said when I'd finished.

I asked, "Are you going to demote me to Better Dresses?"

"What? Oh, Jesus, forget that. I lose my temper quite often."

"Like me, huh?"

He smiled ruefully. "You know, I called your boss to chew him out last night, and he gave me a real talking to. Then I tried to call you to make peace. That must have been when you were out getting mugged by this Frankie."

I remembered the messages he'd left with my answering service. "What did Hank say to you?"

He shook his head. "Ask him about it, if you must know."

I definitely would. Marcus, with his initial hostility and abrupt switch to friendliness, had me puzzled.

Thoughtfully he went on, "This van Osten–Harmon connection throws a new light on my original theory."

"You suspected Charlie Cornish, didn't you?"

"I still do."

So did I. Maybe not of the murder, but of something underhanded. "Why?"

"Initially I had the feeling Cornish was hiding something, so I ran a check on him. You said he was a man without a past, but that's not entirely true."

I felt the sinking sensation that precedes bad news. "What kind of a past does he have?"

"Twenty-four years ago, in his hometown of Ashland,

114

Oregon, Charlie was indicted for arson and murder. The indictment was quashed due to lack of evidence. Right after that, Charlie left town, presumably to come here."

As suspicious of Charlie as I was, I nonetheless came to his defense. "So, on the basis of a dropped charge, you're ready to convict him of the Salem Street arsons and Joan Albritton's murder?"

Marcus held up one hand. "Slow down. I don't want you getting mad at me again. What I'm saying is that the knowledge of his past throws light on certain aspects of Charlie's character, that's all."

"Such as his tendency to set buildings on fire?"

Marcus rolled his eyes toward the ceiling. "What am I going to do with her?" he asked in a hopeless tone, addressing one of the Rembrandts.

I laughed out loud. He reminded me of Joan Albritton, talking to Edwin.

Marcus looked at me with relief. "Well, at least you've got your sense of humor back. For a while, I didn't know if you had one or not. Seriously, Sharon, the charge was arson and *murder*. Charlie's wife and only child died in that fire."

I caught my breath sharply. "No wonder he's buried his past."

"Exactly. And it may have bearing on the present case or it may not. But it does tell you a good deal about why Charlie is the way he is."

I thought of Charlie's little room behind the shop, filled with loneliness and, maybe, an old guilt. I wondered if he had told Joan his secret. With a flash of pity for the big junkman, I understood and excused his deception about the Merchants' Association meeting.

"Anyway," Marcus said briskly, "I'm due at a meeting in half an hour. Since you've taken it this far, what do you plan to do next?"

I was officially back on the case. "Get the truth out of Charlie. You're right about his hiding something, but I don't think he killed Joan. Knowing what you just told me, I think I can force him to talk."

"Good. Let me know."

"I also want to go through Joan's shop again. I finished the inventory before the second break-in, so I may be able to figure out what's missing," I continued. "That could tell us a lot."

He nodded. "Okay, but please be careful. If you like, I'll pick up this Frankie . . ."

"Not yet," I interrupted. "It will tip off Harmon."

"You're probably right." He stood up. "Call me any time, either at the Department or at home. And stay away from Harmon. You know how rough he plays."

I shivered, remembering Frankie's iron grip. "Don't worry!"

We went back through the galleries to the front vestibule, arriving just as Paula emerged from a door marked PRIVATE. I watched Marcus's eyes appraise her and felt a tiny, unreasonable stab of jealousy. He looked at Paula as a woman, a way he'd never looked at me.

Marcus kept on, through the front door, raising a hand in farewell. I watched him run down the steps, his blond hair glinting in the afternoon sun. I had no business getting interested in the man, I told myself sternly.

"Who was that?" Paula's eyes were wide. "You certainly do manage to cram the most into your busy schedule!"

"He's a cop," I said, unwilling to admit what was on my mind, "and up until this afternoon I despised him. I'm sure he'll do something to make me despise him again before the day's over. Now let's go look at those paintings."

116

# Eighteen

Paula suggested we have tea, but I said I didn't have time. As we passed the Japanese Tea Garden, I looked in longingly. Fuschia and lighter-pink flowers bloomed among the carefully sculpted trees and stone lanterns, and gold and white carp swam in the pool. I wished I could take a few minutes to sit in the tea house, drinking from a white porcelain cup.

"You really must be on a case, since you're consorting with cops," Paula said. Paula didn't believe in cops in general and didn't know any in the particular.

"I wasn't exactly consorting. He was there in the museum, and I had to be polite."

"A cultured cop! What next?"

To get the conversation off Marcus, I said, "I've run across stranger things than that in the last few days." I went on to tell her about Joan Albritton's murder and my investigation to date. She listened, occasionally making wry comments, as we walked to where I'd left my car.

When I finished, Paula said, "You do get around. Junk dealers, bail bondsmen, Cara Ingalls. You know, Mrs. Ingalls is on our board—the museum's, I mean. I'd never have the nerve to just approach her like you did. Of course, people who know as much about art as she does always intimidate me."

Paula paused, looking thoughtful. "I could really do some amazing exhibits with some of the stuff from that shop. Can't you see one with a headless dummy walking a stuffed dog? You know, Sharon, this Edwin fellow could be quite valuable. Some of those old department store fittings command high prices. You say he's made of wood?"

"Wooden head, cloth body, and iron shoes."

"I wonder why the shoes? Or, for that matter, why anyone would stuff the family dog. People really do strange things, when you think about it."

"I'd rather not. Think about it, that is." We had gotten to the car, and I unlocked the trunk. "Anyway, here are the paintings." I took them out and propped them on the hood.

Paula bent over, examining them quickly. "Oh, this is Richard's work. Richard Solsby. I'd recognize it anywhere." She looked at me, a wicked little grin on her face. "Richard and I had a thing going back about a year ago, but it wasn't meant to last. There's something curiously limited about a person who can paint only three subjects."

"What do you mean, only three subjects?"

Paula leaned against the car and ticked them off on her fingers. "Still life with flowers and fruit, seascape, street scene. You've got a nice little selection of Richard's work here. We could probably put a show together."

"What about the religious stuff?"

"Religious? Oh, you mean the Madonna and child." She glanced back at the small painting. "That's not Richard's. I got so carried away at seeing his stuff that I overlooked it. You see, I still have an interest in Richard: he owes me fifty dollars, and I'm hoping his work will start to sell."

118

Paula reached for the Madonna and studied it, her face more serious. "No, this definitely isn't Richard's. It's good, almost too good."

"Too good?"

"Yes, much too good." A note of excitement came into her voice. "Sharon, take a look at it. This gold leaf—that's a very old technique, as is painting on wood like this rather than on canvas."

She looked up, then closed her eyes tightly. "Damn it! What am I thinking of?"

"Well, if *you* don't know . . ."

"No. Hush." She held up a hand for quiet, her face intense. "I could swear it's a Bellini. I could swear it! Do you realize you may have been running around with more than a hundred thousand dollars' worth of painting in the trunk of your car?"

"You're kidding!" My knees went weak.

"No, I'm not. Oh, damn! I wish I had my clipping file here with me." Paula looked genuinely distressed.

"Will you please explain from the beginning? What's a Bellini?"

"Bellini," she said, spelling it out, "was a fifteenth-century Italian painter. He did a lot of small altarpieces for wealthy churches. I think this may be part of one."

"Part?"

"Yes. Bellini did his paintings on what is known as a 'triptych'—a three-paneled altarpiece. The sides would depict saints or whatever, with a Madonna and child or a crucifixion at center."

I sighed. "Then I suppose we should get it appraised. It'll really increase the value of Albritton's estate."

"You don't understand," Paula said. "This painting has no business being in this country, much less in a cheap antique shop on Salem Street."

"Why? Joan had some valuable things. They weren't all fakes."

Paula was trembling with excitement. "Sharon, like I said, the Bellini altarpieces were the property of the wealthy

Italian churches. Lately, many of their artworks have been ripped off."

"Then this is a stolen painting?"

She nodded. "I read an article on Italian art thefts a while back. It stuck in my mind, especially the part about the missing Bellini triptych. I cut out the article, and I think I still have it in my file at home."

"My God," I said. "This is a masterpiece?"

"Right. It's also been smuggled into this country. The article said Italian Customs isn't able to stop the paintings from crossing borders and ending up in the hands of private collectors. Some collectors get their kicks from stolen art, even if they have to gloat all alone over what they buy. It's a sickness, like a proverbial miser and his gold. Anyway, this painting somehow has traveled from Italy to Salem Street, and not too long ago. The theft was only last summer."

"From Italy to Salem Street. I wonder if Joan knew she had a masterpiece in her shop." I stopped, aware of the answer to my question. Joan Albritton, a smuggler?

"What a setup!" Paula exclaimed. "A collector could arrange to pick up paintings on Salem Street, and no one would suspect their value. Who would look for real works of art there?"

An ideal setup indeed. How, I wondered, had Joan smuggled them in the first place? "My God," I said softly. I had thought of how Joan had purchased most of her stock.

"Paula," I began, putting it together slowly, "if a painting like this were to come in with a regular shipment of pictures—fake antiques manufactured only last month—would either Italian or American Customs catch it?"

She shook her head. "Not if it was from an established manufacturer. They can't inspect every shipment that goes out. And especially coming into the U.S. they wouldn't."

"Why not?"

"Have you ever seen a ship unload at the docks? A Customs official is there, but usually he doesn't even open the containers. The Customs Bureau has highly trained art experts on its staff, but their job is to recognize fake artworks rather than the real thing."

"I don't understand."

"Fine art—paintings, sculpture, things of obvious merit—is permitted to enter the country duty-free. Promotes culture and so forth. A lot of importers try to pass stuff off as fine art to avoid the duty, and the experts are kept busy detecting fraud. They don't have time to examine every shipment of dutiable merchandise, which your fake antiques would be."

"Then, if the Bellini came from a reputable firm to a known dealer here, if there were periodic shipments from that firm to that dealer, it would probably slip by Customs?"

"I'm sure of it."

I leaned against the car, my mind pushing the facts into place. Joan Albritton and Oliver van Osten: smugglers?

Maybe that was why van Osten looked prosperous. And why Joan had left such a substantial estate.

"Sharon, this painting should not be dragged around this way," Paula was saying. "It's very old and easily damaged by temperature, by just about anything. Why don't I take it into the museum?"

"No," I said. "No, I think I'd better take it to the police. It'll be safe there." I removed it from her hands and got out my car blanket. Even with the Bellini wrapped inside, it would still look like a standard issue U.S. Navy blanket. I stowed it and the other paintings away. Paula watched me as if I were locking a baby in the trunk.

"Could you find me that article on the thefts?" I asked her.

"Sure. I'll look for it as soon as I get home."

"I'd really appreciate that."

"No trouble. I'd like a few paintings left in the churches if I ever visit Italy again."

I grinned at her and got in the car. "Thanks for your help. I'll call you." As I drove off, I could see Paula standing in the road, waving at me and the Bellini.

The next step, I thought, was to look at van Osten's

catalogues to see if he imported paintings from any Italian firms. That meant I should pay his office a visit—but after business hours. In the meantime, I'd track down Charlie Cornish and demand the truth about his peculiar behavior.

# Nineteen

Tracking down Charlie proved to be a problem. Junk Emporium was still locked up tight, so I went down the block to Dan Efron's shop. Dan was busy extolling the merits of an old gas stove to a customer, so I had to wait. The stove looked even more decrepit than the one in my apartment, but Dandy made it sound like a real find.

When the customer had paid for the stove and hauled it to a waiting van, Dan turned to me, a foolish grin on his face.

"How's Austin getting along, Dan?" I asked, remembering I had left the little shopkeeper in his possession the night before.

The grin faded. "Oh, not so good. I got him home all right, and his missus made sure he had a couple of stiff drinks, but she says he's really down in the dumps today. Has to see the insurance people, and you can bet they'll try to screw him out of every cent they can."

I sighed. "Poor Austin. Have you seen Charlie around by any chance?"

Dan looked even gloomier. "That's another one of us who's not in great shape."

"I saw his shop was closed up."

"Yeah, first time I can remember it being. I'm afraid Charlie's hitting the bottle pretty hard."

"You mean he's in there drinking?"

Dan shook his head. "Nope. He stopped by about an hour ago, wanted to know if I'd go down to the Lucky Lounge for a few beers. I would've, but I couldn't leave the store."

I asked, "Where's the Lucky Lounge?"

"Over on McAllister Street. But you wouldn't want to go there."

"Why not?"

Dan looked embarrassed. "Well, the kind of women they get in there, they're not what I'd call your class."

"Don't worry, Dan. If anybody offers me money, I won't get offended."

"Aw, they're not all whores." He scratched his head in confusion. "Some of them're just old drunks."

I left Dan in front of his shop, his grin back in place, and walked over to McAllister Street. The Lucky Lounge was a standard working-class bar; its neon sign advertised hours from six A.M., the earliest city ordinance permitted drinks to be served. I pushed open the door and entered a gloomy room.

A bar with cracked leather stools ran along the left side, and small booths lined the wall on the right. A jukebox was playing a country song about "the most beautiful girl in the world." In the far booth, Charlie sat hunched over a shell of light beer.

"Can I help you, ma'am?" A voice spoke from behind the bar. I gestured toward Charlie and kept going.

When I got to the booth, Charlie looked up. Although his eyes were red, I could tell he hadn't been drinking heavily. He just looked like a lonely old man nursing a single beer.

"Are you going to ask me to join you?" I tried to make my

124

voice stern, but it was difficult. I'd developed a certain affection for Charlie Cornish despite the trouble he'd caused me.

He gestured at the side of the booth opposite him. "Can't see why you'd want to, but go ahead. I'll even buy you a beer."

I sat down, and he signaled to a tired-looking waitress, who leaned against the bar, resting her feet. She brought another glass of beer and set it in front of me, giving me a curious glance. Charlie and I didn't look like a particularly well-suited couple.

"I guess you want some sort of explanation," Charlie said, "about why I never asked the Association to hire you, I mean."

"I had thought of asking for one, yeah."

"That's what I was afraid of. You ask too damn many questions." He tried to smile at me, but it didn't come off.

The jukebox stopped playing, and Charlie picked a couple of quarters out of the change on the table and went to make more selections. I waited. I had plenty of time to hear what he had to tell me.

He came back and sat down heavily. The same song played over again.

" '. . . woke up this morning, realized what I'd done. I stood alone in the cold gray dawn, knew I'd lost my morning sun.' " Charlie sang along, slightly off key. " 'Heeeey, did you happen to see the most beautiful girl in the world? . . .' "

I started to smile. Joan Albritton had been neither beautiful nor a girl. Then I stopped, aware of the tendency when one is still young to assume that all life and passion stop with the onset of gray hair. To Charlie, Joan had perhaps been exactly what the song said. His world would forever be diminished now.

"So go ahead and ask me why I didn't do it," he said suddenly, in mid-song.

I shook my head. "I think I know. You were afraid I'd find out too much."

He looked at me keenly. "Too much about what?"

"About your past, maybe. About what really happened that night when you went over to Joan's shop." The last was a shot in the dark, based on his recent guilt-stricken behavior.

It hit home. His face crumpled, and he dug his fingers into his palms. "You think you know so much, you tell me."

"I know how your wife and child died. How they indicted you for it. Did Joan know?"

"She knew. It never made any difference to her ... at least, I never thought it did until Monday night. I thought she understood."

"Understood what? Did you really kill them?"

He shrugged, hopeless pain on his face. "I always thought I did. I can half-remember dropping a cigarette into the pile of cleaning rags that started the fire. But then, I was never sure whether I did it that day or any one of a hundred other days, or if the cigarette was even lit. It's always been hazy, but God knows I could have done it. I loved my wife, but she didn't love me, and the kid wasn't even mine."

It made me hurt, his living a life filled with guilt for something he wasn't even sure he'd done. "Did Joan throw it up to you on Monday night?"

He nodded. "I went to see her. I wanted to try to talk her out of selling to Ben Harmon."

"Then you knew about her agreement with him before he came to see you the other night?"

"Not really, but I kind of suspected it. The way he'd been hanging around her, I knew he was after her property. He had her fooled, so I tried to shock her back to her senses."

"How?"

"By telling her Harmon was responsible for the arsons and vandalisms."

"Was he?"

Charlie gestured wearily. "I think so. I saw one of his henchmen, that little skinny one they call Frankie, around right before a couple of the fires. Harmon can get that little creep to do any kind of dirty work."

126

Silently I agreed. "So you told Joan that?"

"Right. She blew up at me, told me I was trying to smear Harmon out of jealousy for their friendship. She reminded me of how I'd been indicted for arson. Said I should look to myself first."

I sucked in my breath.

"Then," Charlie went on, "I did the thing I'm so ashamed of. I hit her, slapped her really hard."

I remembered the mention of a bruise in the medical examiner's report.

"It was horrible, Sharon. She just stood there, her hand to her face for a few minutes. And then she took the little chain off her neck and unlocked that cabinet. She got my locket out—the silver locket I bought her twenty years ago when I told her about my past and she said that it didn't matter, that she loved me anyway."

He fumbled at the neck of his fatigues and brought it out, an old-fashioned silver filigree heart. "She gave it back to me and said—I'll never forget her face when she said it—she said, 'You're nothing to me now. You're nothing.'"

His voice broke, and he leaned his head on his fist. I reached across and took his other hand, unlocking the clenched fingers and smoothing them out on the table.

"When I went back," his muffled voice said, "when I went back to ask her to forgive me, she was dead."

I didn't say anything, just sat there, my hand on his. It must have been five minutes before he raised his head.

"So now you know. I was afraid you might find out I'd been over there and fought with her. That police lieutenant had already been snooping around—I think he knows about me—and I was scared. So scared for my own stupid hide that I put it before finding Joanie's killer."

I cleared my throat, finding it hard to speak. "Okay. Okay, Charlie. But you're not doing that any more, and I think I'm getting closer to him."

A little interest flickered in his dull eyes. "Really?"

I hesitated. I didn't want to further burden him with the

knowledge that his dead love, in all likelihood, had been a crook. Finally I said, "I want to ask you one more question, and then I'll go."

"All right."

"Was there ever a time in the last few years when Joan needed money, more money than she could get out of the shop?"

He looked puzzled. "Not that I know ... oh, wait a minute. Of course. The kid."

"Her grandson?"

"Right. Christopher. He was a hell of a talented musician and had already been accepted at Juilliard when he was only a junior in high school—some sort of early-decision plan for gifted kids. Joanie worried that she wouldn't be able to send him. She didn't want to see his talent go to waste like hers did when she married her no-good bum of a husband and dropped out of art school."

"What did she do about it?"

"Do?" He gave me a blank look. "Not much, as I recall. She stopped worrying, cut down on expenses, and put money away. And the kid got the part-time job with the rock group."

"When was this, Charlie? Think hard."

He frowned. "As near as I remember, it was the fall of Chris's junior year. That would be a year ago last fall. Chris was supposed to leave for New York this past August, if he got off on the drug charge."

That meant a year and a half ago Joan had been ripe for a money-making scheme. The intrigue of belonging to a smuggling ring might have even excited her.

I stood up, setting my untouched beer in front of Charlie.

"Where are you going now?" he asked.

"Downtown, for a while. I'll be in touch with you. I'll let you know as soon as I find the killer." I started to go, then added, "And, Charlie, if that Lieutenant Marcus comes around, tell him exactly what you told me. He's a reasonable man; he'll believe you." I hurried out of the bar.

128

What I'd said was true: Marcus, when he wasn't putting on a big, fiery, official policeman show, could be very reasonable indeed. That didn't apply to what I was planning, however. If Marcus knew I was about to break into Oliver van Osten's office, the cop show would be staged with full pyrotechnics.

# Twenty

Having worked in security myself, I knew getting past a guard was largely a matter of observing his routines and finding a weak spot. I stationed myself at the trolley stop in front of the old building on Market Street where van Osten had his office and watched the man in uniform.

It was close to seven in the evening, but a large number of people were going into the building. The guard asked each his or her name and checked it off on a list. At seven sharp, about twenty people showed up at once, and a line formed. I crossed the sidewalk and attached myself to the end.

"Organizational behavior," a woman in front of me was saying to the man with her, "is the worst course this school offers. I'm taking it because it's required for the degree."

"I'm taking it," the man said, "to get out of the house one night a week."

It explained the crowd. Golden Gate University, a downtown institution specializing in business and law, held many of its night classes in space donated by local companies. Some firm in van Osten's building must have an organizational behavior class meeting in its conference room; the list the security guard consulted was probably the student roster. I hoped someone had cut class tonight.

As I neared the guard, I watched him check off the people in front of me. He didn't ask for identification, but I could tell he wasn't familiar with their faces because he barely looked up. A little Sony TV stood on the desk, the volume down. The guard probably was anxious to get back to his program.

When my turn came, I scanned the printed list, then pointed to a name that wasn't checked. It was short and easy to read upside down.

"That's it," I said. "Milne."

The guard grunted and marked it off. I followed the others to the elevator, and we rode to the twelfth floor. There, I started off the other way from my companions, making vague noises about the ladies' room.

The woman who was taking the course because it was required called to me, "You'll have to go down a flight. They only have one on every other floor."

"Thanks." I went through the exit door, where I wanted to go anyway.

Van Osten's card said his office was number 602. I went down to the sixth floor. It was quiet, and no lights shone through the pebbled-glass doors. I went along to the right office. I could break the glass to get in, but I hoped I wouldn't have to. From my bag, I took the set of passkeys I'd acquired over the years. The lock yielded on the eighth try.

Inside I paused, listening to the silence, then took out my pencil flash and shone it around a standard reception room with standard office furniture. The walls were an uninteresting beige, and the desk and side chair were that yellow oak I remembered from grade school. No attempt had been made at decoration save a vase of red carnations on the desk, which only made the room more wretched by comparison. I guessed van Osten didn't care to spend money on his office, since he was out much of the time calling on his customers. I moved past the desk and through a connecting door. All was quiet there, too.

Three other doors opened off the small hallway where I stood. The first revealed only a supply closet. The next led into a showroom with samples of antiques scattered about. A bookcase held several shelves of bound notebooks, probably the manufacturers' catalogues.

I shone my light on them, bypassing those with English, French, or German names, until I came to one on the second shelf labeled GIANNINI & BANDUCCI, INC. Taking it to a nearby table, I leafed through it, looking at the illustrations. Giannini & Banducci manufactured a great many paintings.

I turned the pages faster until I came to an illustration of a doleful-eyed Madonna and child. To my unschooled eyes, it was not very different from the Bellini in the trunk of my car. The accompanying description read: "Fifty assorted religious paintings in the Florentine style. Order No. BX1731."

The number caught my notice. I rummaged through my bag for the notebook where I'd copied the information from Joan's ledger that morning. BX1731 was the shipment that should have arrived last Monday; maybe it had arrived after all. If so, where were the other forty-nine paintings?

I went looking for number CD1910, the other order I'd noted from the ledger. It appeared on page 231, illustrated by a sorrowing Mary at the foot of the cross. "Fifty assorted oil paintings, Late Gothic."

That was an awful lot of religious paintings for one small shop, especially a shop slated to relocate soon. Putting the catalogue back on the shelf, I left the showroom and opened the third door.

Van Osten certainly didn't waste any money on frills. The office contained a functional oak desk and a row of steel filing cabinets. I located a drawer marked PURCHASE OR-DERS—G & B.

In a few minutes, I had the order for the Florentine

religious paintings, stamped "Received by Customer," with Monday's date. Van Osten's secretary kept her files current.

A second purchase order, for the Late Gothic paintings, showed the shipment due to arrive tomorrow and gave the name of a freight forwarder. A handwritten note indicated the delivery instructions had been changed on Tuesday of this week. The order was to go directly to van Osten Imports rather than Joan's Unique Antiques. I copied the information by the light of my flash.

I knew how the smuggling was done now, but I finished searching the office. It told nothing else; van Osten, like most salesmen, probably carried important papers in his briefcase. I went through the secretary's desk next and came up empty-handed. Finally I rechecked the supply closet.

The box sat on the floor as if it were waiting for me. Its shipping label bore the return address of Giannini & Banducci, Roma, Italia, and delivery instructions to Joan's Unique Antiques, San Francisco, California, U.S.A.

Inside, it was packed with small religious paintings. When I lifted one out, I could immediately tell the difference, in both weight and quality, between it and the Bellini. I knelt down and counted the paintings.

There were forty-nine. Joan must have taken one out and hung it on the wall of the shop next to Edwin, where the killer missed it. The box was what he had taken the night of the murder. And the Bellini was what he had returned for. Returned, only to find it gone.

Fear stabbed at me, and I stood up, listening to the quiet, which, if I let it, was going to start seeming tangible and ominous. It was time I got out of there, and quickly. The pieces of my theory about the murder were falling into place.

# Twenty-one

I stopped at a pay phone on Market Street and called police headquarters. Marcus was off duty but had left his home number for me. I called it and said I wanted to talk to him right away. He suggested I come to his place and gave me instructions.

Twenty minutes later, I parked on Twin Peaks in front of a small redwood house that seemed to cling to the slope of the hill behind it. I went up and rang the bell. Footsteps descended from the second floor, a light flashed on, and Greg Marcus opened the door. He was dressed in Levi's, his feet in soft leather moccasins.

He gave me a penetrating glance and gestured for me to come in. "Well, papoose, don't tell me you've solved the case already."

The nickname annoyed me, but I let it go. "Practically. I've uncovered some complicating factors."

"Just what I need. I don't suppose I can bribe you to go home and mind your own business?"

"You tried that yesterday."

"That was a threat, not a bribe."

We were standing in a large entryway that seemed to take up half the ground floor. The other half would probably be a garage, and the living space would be on the second and third floors. I saw that one wall was covered by a mural, a wheat-colored hillside dotted with dark green trees.

"That's a nice mural," I commented.

"Thank you. It was done by a friend, the artistic one I was talking about before. She did a good Cézanne." He turned and led me upstairs to the living room.

At the back, the room opened into a lush, floodlit garden of shrubs and vines that cascaded down from the hillside. Toward the front, the lights of the city spread beyond picture windows. Logs blazed cheerfully in a fireplace at one end, where a couple of easy chairs and a long, low table were drawn up. On the table sat an earthenware teapot and two cups.

"This is a great house," I said. "Your garden is beautiful."

"Glad you like it. My ex-wife did most of the planting. I seem to attract women who enjoy making home improvements."

"How nice for you," I said with dry emphasis.

Marcus ignored my sarcasm. "Say, you and I could become lovers, and then you could add something to the house, too."

I stared at him.

"Don't look so horrified. I've been told I'm not all that bad. How would you improve this room?"

"With a gun collection." I could feel the .38 in my bag, where I'd put it that morning.

"It's the little feminine touches that make a home," Marcus said.

We grinned at each other warily. Our brief acquaintanceship had taken an unexpected turn.

"Thought maybe you could use some tea," Marcus said, waving me into one of the chairs. "I was just going to toast myself a bagel when you called. Want one? With cream cheese?"

I thought back to the cannelloni I'd had at lunch with Cara Ingalls. "I'd love one. As usual, I've forgotten to eat."

He laughed and disappeared into the adjoining kitchen.

I sat down in front of the fire, trying to find a way to make my tale of art theft and smuggling sound credible. When Marcus returned with bagels smothered in cream cheese, I practically leaped at mine, not caring if I looked starved.

Still hoping I'd have a brainstorm about how to present my theory, I stalled for time. "What happened to your wife?"

Marcus looked surprised. "I guess being a private eye gives you an excuse for your nosiness. She got tired of being married to a dumb cop and went off to law school. She even did our own divorce."

He didn't look too upset about it. And he wasn't a dumb cop by any means. "And your arty friend?"

"I rejected her proposal to make an honest man out of me, and she went off in a huff."

"Of course. Ladies don't like to be turned down." I munched on the bagel, licking my fingertips as politely as I could. Marcus watched me, amusement glinting in his eyes.

I imagined my mother's horror if she knew her well-bred daughter was talking to a cop with her mouth full. My mother had a deeply ingrained respect for good table manners . . . and the law. When I had finished the bagel, I said, "The murderer is Oliver van Osten."

Marcus stared at me. "The antique dealer?"

I corrected him. "Fake-antique dealer."

"Right. Fake-antique dealer. What do you base this on?"

I explained about van Osten's business, Joan's purchases from him, and the presence of a stolen masterpiece in the Salem Street shop. When I got to the method of smuggling the paintings inside shipments of commercially dutiable fakes, Marcus leaned forward with interest.

"Van Osten has a European accomplice," I said, "probably someone with the Italian firm, who receives the stolen paintings and slips them into the shipments to Joan. Customs doesn't catch it because they're looking for fakes masquerading as the real thing.

"The way I figure it, when the paintings arrived at Salem Street, Joan would notify van Osten, who in turn would tell the collectors to pick them up. None of the smuggled artworks ever entered van Osten's office, thus keeping him one step removed from the operation. An importer would be suspect, but not a cheap antique shop."

"Given all this," Marcus said, "why would Joan Albritton get involved in such a thing?"

"Because she needed money to send her grandson East to music school. And, from what I gather, Joan was a romantic. The idea of smuggling may have appealed to her fanciful side."

Marcus nodded thoughtfully. "So far so good. But why did she keep on doing it after the kid died?"

"I think at first she felt she was in too deep to pull out," I said. "But then the buildings were condemned, and she knew she had to move. Charlie said she'd spoken of retiring. Van Osten may have killed her for backing out of the operation."

Marcus shook his head. "I think he'd be able to find someone else to receive the stuff. Killing Joan would be too great a risk and serve no real purpose."

"Maybe not, but there's another factor. Van Osten may have thought she would double-cross him on the property deal."

"The property deal? You didn't mention van Osten had bid for the land."

"He hadn't, not directly. But I think he and Ben Harmon were partners. Harmon, with the same general set of plans as the Ingalls syndicate, was going to lease Joan a shop at a reduced rent, remember? She, in turn, could bring in a lot more stock and, naturally, a lot more stolen paintings."

Marcus grunted. "Then Harmon may be involved in the smuggling, too."

"Probably not from the first, but he could have found out about it from Joan when he started spending time with her after Christopher's death. Then he could have pressured van Osten to give him a piece of the action."

"You think Harmon was after those properties all along? Could he have gotten that much money together? For real?"

"Who knows? But I'm pretty sure he was responsible for the original arsons, although he did his best to implicate the Western Addition Credit Union. Charlie thinks so, too: he saw our friend Frankie around when a couple of the fires started."

"So why, if the deal was set, did Harmon throw bricks at Charlie's shop the other night?"

"He didn't. As I said this afternoon, that was the murderer's way of getting me out of the shop so he could take the Bellini. It was van Osten who threw the bricks; I recognized him when I saw his silhouette on the draperies at his apartment. I think he also set Bigby's shop on fire to decoy your man away from Joan's. Since there had been a rash of vandalisms before, people would naturally think these were more of the same."

"This is far-fetched enough to be true," Marcus said. "Where does Cornish fit in?"

"He doesn't." I repeated Charlie's confession about the night of Joan's murder.

"Poor devil," Marcus commented when I finished. "No one makes up a pitiful story like that. But back to van Osten: Why didn't he take the Bellini with him that night and save himself all the trouble?"

"He tried. He took the carton with the other paintings, but Joan had already removed the Bellini and hung it on the wall by Edwin, the mannequin with the iron shoes. That's another possible reason for her murder: she may have held out on the Bellini. Why else would she have hung it up?"

Marcus gave me a sharp look. "You haven't given me any concrete proof. How do you know he took that box?"

"I saw it. It's in the supply closet at his office, and his records show it was delivered to Joan's shop on Monday."

He frowned. "I suppose," he said, "that you saw his records, too?"

"Well . . ."

He held up a hand. "Don't tell me; I don't want to know. But with the presence of the box, plus his records, you may have concrete evidence after all."

"There's more evidence coming, too. A second shipment is due tomorrow. The delivery instructions were originally to Joan's shop, but van Osten changed them on Tuesday, to his office." I took my notebook out and read off the particulars.

Marcus looked at me with excitement. "Good work! We'll have to move in on van Osten's office before he destroys that box or his records. And I'll get in touch with Customs and arrange to examine this second shipment as soon as . . ." The muffled ring of the telephone cut him off. He got up and went into the kitchen.

I leaned back and watched the fire, full of self-satisfaction. The case was virtually wrapped up.

Marcus's voice spoke behind me. "If van Osten murdered Joan Albritton, justice has already been meted out."

I turned to face him. "What do you mean?"

He was reaching into a small closet for his trench coat while slipping out of his moccasins and into street shoes. "Van Osten's dead. Murdered at his apartment. I'm going over there."

I stared at him, then stood up, gathering my purse and jacket.

"Where do you think you're going?" Marcus asked.

"I thought . . . well, I could go home or . . ."

"Or come with me." He regarded me with a bemused

expression, then shrugged. "Oh, what the hell. I never knew a young woman with such a fondness for looking at dead bodies, but if that's what you want to do, come on along."

# Twenty-two

When we arrived at the brown-shingled building on Point Lobos Avenue, Marcus double-parked next to a blue-and-white cruiser. I jumped out of the car and hurried after him. I didn't want to lose him; he was my entrée to the murder scene.

The front door of the building stood open, and bystanders, many of them in bathrobes, were milling about. Marcus pushed through the crowd, and I followed in his wake. He took the carpeted stairs two at a time, following the sound of activity. I kept close behind.

In apartment five, officials and lab technicians bustled about. My eyes immediately went to the sheeted figure on the floor and the blood spatters on the pale-yellow carpet. There was a great deal of blood. I stopped in the doorway, drawing in my breath.

Marcus turned, noticing me for the first time, and gestured for me to come in.

"I trust you know enough to keep out of the way and not touch anything."

I nodded.

"Good." He dropped a hand onto my shoulder and gave it a brief squeeze, then turned to a man in civilian clothes who had approached him. From the way he addressed Marcus, this was one of the detectives on his squad. I looked around while the two men talked.

The room was furnished in a combination of functional modern pieces and antiques, the latter strategically placed to call attention to themselves. Van Osten's taste in home decorating, unlike that of his office, had been impeccable, but tonight the room looked as though it had been sacked by a roving army of Huns.

Drawers stood open, stuffing bled from gaping wounds in the upholstery, pictures hung at odd angles. Even the wastebasket had been emptied, its contents scattered on the floor, mingling with the blood. It reminded me of the destruction at Joan's shop.

Marcus turned back to me and said in a low voice, "It's the same M.O. as the Albritton killing, and the medical examiner says the wound could have been caused by the same weapon. From the blood-spatter pattern, he must have fallen forward after he was stabbed, then tried to crawl after his attacker. The wound is to the jugular, which is why there's so much blood."

I swallowed, my throat dry. "That long blade would make it an easy job."

"Right," he said. "Whoever it was, he knew what he was doing. It's a single wound, nice and clean."

"Van Osten must have known him then. I don't think he was the sort to let strangers get too close to him. Could he have surprised someone in the process of searching?"

"Doubt it. Neighbors say he was here all evening, and the stereo was on."

144

I asked, "Who found him?"

"Woman across the hall. Evidently they were close friends. She came over to ask him to have a drink with her. The FM was playing, but he didn't answer the door. She got worried and used her key." Marcus glanced at the stereo setup on the wall. "Hey, Gallagher," he said to the other detective, "what volume was that thing at?"

"Around five."

Marcus nodded. "That's loud enough to cover up most ordinary sounds."

He moved toward the body. I hung back, then followed unwillingly.

Marcus lifted the corner of the sheet, and I saw van Osten, sprawled forward, his head twisted to one side, hand reaching out in a last desperate grasp. His face was rigid with horror, the eyes frozen. Even in death, he did not manage to convey anything with those eyes.

I took a deep, shaky breath, and Marcus looked at me. "You all right?"

I was trembling and afraid I would start to hyperventilate. I forced myself to take shallow, well-spaced breaths. "I'll be okay."

He flashed a look of quick understanding and lowered the sheet. "Don't like dead bodies as much as you thought you did?" he asked gently.

"I've never liked them, and I've seen quite a few."

"Neither have I." He guided me away from the body, then went up to Gallagher and questioned him about the neighbors.

Gallagher said none of them had heard anything. "The grove of trees across the street screens the building pretty well. With the overlook to Seal Rock and the Cliff House, plus the motel on the other corner, the residents don't take much notice of strangers or strange cars."

I asked, "What about familiar cars? No one noticed a person who visited here frequently?"

Gallagher looked at me in surprise. He was an earnest,

owlish young man, and it clearly bothered him that he couldn't figure out what I was doing there. After a few seconds he replied in the negative.

When Marcus glanced at me, there was a glimmer of amusement in his eyes. Then he said, "You're thinking the same thing I am?"

"Right. Van Osten's probable partner has been here at least once that I know of, maybe many times more. He would suspect that van Osten had the Bellini. Look at the way the paintings have been cut: it's a careful job." I crossed to one hanging askew on the far wall and indicated the slashes.

Marcus nodded. "Someone didn't want to harm whatever might be concealed there."

We stood, looking at the canvas in silence.

"All right," Marcus said briskly. "Gallagher's got everything under control. I suggest we go interview the girlfriend, this Dorothy Brosig."

We crossed to the opposite apartment. A small, dark-haired woman in a blue chenille bathrobe sat on the couch, her head bowed. Her hands were clasped in her lap, her slippered feet drawn tightly together. She raised a tear-stained face as we approached her, and I saw she was in her early thirties and attractive in a severe way. Three or four people who were clustered around the couch began to withdraw from the room.

"Ms. Brosig?" Marcus's voice was kind. "I'm Lieutenant Marcus of Homicide and this is Ms. McCone. We'd like to ask you a few questions."

She shrugged wearily. "I've already told the other detective everything that happened, but go ahead, if you must."

"Thank you." Marcus sat down on the couch, and I perched on the edge of a nearby chair. "Did you expect to see Mr. van Osten tonight?"

She sighed. "We didn't have any specific plans, but we usually got together for a drink or two."

"So far as you know, Mr. van Osten was planning to spend the evening at home, alone?"

146

"No. I thought he'd had an appointment, but he must not have. His lights were on, and the music was playing when I got home."

"When was that?"

"Around nine. I'd been working overtime—I'm a secretary at Crocker Bank—and I'd brought some carry-out from McDonald's. I ate, then changed and went over to see Oliver but . . . but he was dead." Tears filled her eyes but did not spill over.

Marcus nodded sympathetically. "What made you think Mr. van Osten had an evening appointment?"

"I'm not certain. I just guessed he had one from what he said this afternoon when he called me at work. You see, we had plans for a trip to Mexico, and I was supposed to make arrangements through the bank's travel agent. Oliver called and said to hold off because he had a deal to close, and he wasn't sure how long it would take. He said he might know where he stood tonight, and certainly by the weekend. I assumed he must be meeting with someone."

Marcus and I exchanged glances. The final shipment to Joan Albritton would be here by the weekend.

"Did he mention what kind of deal?" Marcus asked Dorothy Brosig.

She shook her head. "We didn't discuss his business much. I don't even know his customers, except for the old lady."

"The old lady?" Marucs glanced at me.

"The one who got herself killed the other night. I didn't really know her, just of her. Oliver said she was a big customer, and he stood to lose a lot because she died." Dorothy Brosig frowned. "And then he said this other thing, about when you're handed a lemon you should squeeze it and make lemonade. That's what he was going to do, he said, make lemonade out of the old lady's death."

"Did you ask him what he meant by that?"

"Oh, no!" Dorothy Brosig looked shocked. "It wasn't my business. You see, Oliver likes . . . liked to talk, but he didn't really talk for my benefit."

She was a perfect woman for van Osten: obedient, incurious, and really not too bright. I revised my earlier theory. It now sounded like van Osten had not killed Joan but had known who did.

Marcus continued questioning the woman: Had she seen anyone tonight, heard anything? Who were van Osten's friends? What had his emotional state been lately? What shape were his finances in? The answers yielded nothing.

Finally Marcus stood up, and I followed suit. He went through the usual formalities about getting in touch if she remembered anything, and then we left the building. The crowds outside had dispersed.

In the car, Marcus sat tapping the steering wheel with his fingers for a full minute. Finally he asked me, "You changing your mind, too?"

"You mean, do I think Ben Harmon killed both of them? I don't know."

Marcus looked thoughtful for a few seconds, then said, "Well, I'll have my men move in on van Osten's office tonight, and tomorrow I'll get in touch with our friendly Customs inspector and meet that shipment at the dock. I'll check it out to confirm the smuggling, then pick up Harmon. He may cave in when he realizes we're onto his involvement with van Osten. I'd sure like to find that bone-handled knife on him."

He started the car and turned back up Point Lobos toward town. I suddenly felt exhausted and dozed, just a little, as he drove to Twin Peaks.

"Want to come in for a drink?" he asked as he turned into the driveway of the little redwood house.

I paused, then shook my head. "A drink would finish me. I need some sleep."

He looked at me, a long, speculative look, then moved over, as if to open my door. He stopped, his arm resting around my shoulders.

"When this thing is wrapped up," he said, "I'd like to see you again, nonprofessionally. I can teach you all about Rembrandt and Cézanne and . . ." he hesitated.

148

I tilted my head back to look at him. His eyes were serious. "And?"

"And there are things you can teach me, too." It came out almost grudgingly.

I wanted to smile, but I realized what he wanted to say was coming hard to him. "Such as?"

"Things about a strong man and a strong woman ..." he paused again, his eyes intent on mine. "About how two such people can be together without diminishing each other or tearing each other apart."

I smiled. "I'd be willing to try."

His kiss was an offering, not a demand. I accepted.

I leaned my head against his arm, exhaustion and desire mingling. Like me, however, Greg was unable to remain on his good behavior for long. He moved his lips close to my right ear and whispered, "My God, papoose. I can't tell whether you're succumbing to my charms or falling asleep!"

I jerked away, glaring. "For a detective, you're not very observant. And will you quit calling me that ridiculous name? It's a racial slur!"

He burst out laughing and moved away. "When you think about it, it's also sexist and agist."

I opened the door and got out of the car. Greg followed.

"The course of our relationship is not destined to run smoothly." He was standing on the sidewalk, the old sarcastic grin on his face.

"I'm sure you're right!" I got into my car, slipped on the seatbelt, and started up. Aloud I muttered, "If anyone had told me two nights ago that I'd ever let that bastard kiss me, I'd have said they were insane!"

Then I made a U-turn, right there under the eyes of the law, and drove home to bed.

# *Twenty-three*

I couldn't sleep the whole night. As soon as I found a parking space near my building, Paula's comment about over a hundred thousand dollars' worth of painting came back to me. I removed the Bellini from the trunk and, with it still wrapped in the blanket, hurried furtively down the sidewalk.

Why hadn't I turned it over to Greg as I'd intended? I supposed the shock of our prime suspect's murder had driven the thought of the stolen masterpiece from our heads. I fumbled with my keys, glancing over my shoulder.

Inside, I unwrapped the painting and set it on a chair. The Madonna and child glowed at me, luminous and rounded against the gold leaf. I admired it until footsteps in the alley jerked me back to reality.

Footsteps in the alley were perfectly normal. It was a convenient, well-traveled shortcut through the neighborhood, and I usually paid no attention to passers-by. But then I didn't usually have a Bellini in my apartment. I wrapped the Madonna again and stuffed it under the bed. Anyone who wanted it would have to disturb me first. I undressed and got under the covers.

And tossed and turned. God, how I tossed and turned! The act of sleeping on top of a potential fortune made me a veritable gyroscope.

Through the night, my mind wandered from the Bellini to the new relationship I seemed to have contracted with the lieutenant. Contracted was a good word for it, too: as in contracting a disease, I didn't think it would be healthy. Greg Marcus was a headstrong, domineering man, and I was an equally self-willed woman. He might talk of two such people co-existing in harmony, but I suspected he and I were more the tearing-apart type.

Around three in the morning I heard noises outside again and spent a bad hour wondering if Harmon's Spanish thug had returned. If Harmon had ordered Frankie to commit the Salem Street arsons, he could also have ordered him to kill van Osten, or to kill me. By morning, my nerves were a mess.

At nine thirty I was about to call Greg, hoping if he picked up the Bellini he'd take me along to the docks. As I reached for the phone, it rang. The ship, Greg said, was at Pier 97. A Customs inspector would meet him there at eleven. Did I want to come with him?

Of course I did! I abandoned the coffee I'd been nursing and got dressed.

Twenty minutes later my bell rang. I buzzed back and opened the door to Greg, striding across the lobby, looking fresh and cheerful.

"Morning." He dropped a kiss on the top of my head and walked into the apartment with an air of confident possession. I followed, my eyes narrowed.

"Nice place, for a papoose." He examined my picturesque alley view, then turned and saw my face. "Uh, oh. Don't go getting mad at me. It's too early in the day. Where's the Bellini?"

"Under my bed."

"What is it doing under your bed?"

"I hid it there last night. Then I couldn't sleep."

He grinned. "You don't look too well rested. I thought, until you mentioned it on the phone this morning, that it was safely stored at the de Young. If I'd known you had it, I'd have kept it myself, but then *I* wouldn't have slept."

"Always look out for Number One," I muttered and went to get the painting.

Greg took the bundle and unwrapped it. He whistled softly. "God, it *is* the real thing! No wonder you were nervous."

"You can tell, just like that?"

He shrugged. "I couldn't have identified it as a Bellini if I hadn't had Files locate a copy of that article your friend told you about first thing this morning. There was an illustration of the stolen triptych, and this looks like part of it. But the quality of this is what makes me sure. It has an aura . . ." He stopped. "You must think I'm peculiar, a cop who's an art lover."

It was what Paula had said the day before. "I admit you've challenged my stereotypes."

"Well, I had a good tutor, and I've continued to explore the field on my own." Momentarily he looked pensive. Then he said, "Let's get going."

Pier 97 loomed up as we drove in, enveloping us in its gloom. Customs Inspector Ed Windfeldt, a tall, graying man with a grim, traplike mouth, had met us outside and slipped into the car beside me. Now he flashed his badge at the uniformed guard, who waved us toward a parking space inside the pier.

As we got out of the car, Windfeldt said curtly, "Wait here. I'll go present the search warrant and see if they've located the container." Even the set of his shoulders was grim as he walked away from us.

I leaned back against the car and looked up at the arching roof of the pier. It was a huge, towering structure, jammed with vehicles and cargo. Huge wooden containers piled one on the other, and forklifts zipped among the stacks. The sounds of engines and dockworkers' voices echoed in the chill air.

I shivered, more from excitement than cold.

Greg looked at me in understanding. "It's not long now. Makes it all worth it when everything starts coming together, doesn't it?"

"Yes."

"Even getting knocked around by Frankie?"

"Sure."

"And being yelled at by pushy cops?"

"Even that."

His eyes watched me carefully. "Private eyes are funny people."

"So are pushy cops."

"You're right there. Ever think of becoming a cop?"

"I did, but at the time there wasn't much opportunity for women. Lady cops were confined to typing, taking shorthand, and the juvenile division."

"And I don't suppose you have any womanly skills like typing and shorthand?"

I smiled. "No, but I'm a mean shot with a .38, and I bake terrific bread."

He smiled back, getting the message. "If you'll bake me some, I'll take you to the police range next week."

"It's a deal."

"Rye, with caraway seeds on top?"

"Sure." I saw Inspector Windfeldt coming toward us and turned to watch him.

"They've located the container," he said, "but it'll take them a while to get at the particular carton. Come this way."

He led us through the stacks of cargo, stopping to let a loaded forklift go by. I wondered if the Customs inspector was always so curt, or if he was embarrassed at our discovery of the smuggling operation.

Windfeldt stopped at an immense wooden crate, motioning to a couple of stevedores working nearby. They approached, crowbars in hand.

The crate was over eight feet tall and six feet wide. I asked Greg, "How are they going to find one box in that thing?"

"Don't ask me. I'm new to this game, too."

The stevedores attacked the crate, prying at the side nearest us. I stepped back as the wood splintered and the side gave way, crashing to the concrete floor. Greg put his hand on my shoulder, tense fingers digging in. I glanced up at his face. He looked as impatient as I felt.

"Whole goddamn case depends on one little painting in all of that." He rubbed the back of his neck.

Windfeldt stepped forward, consulting a bill of lading, and began examining the shipping instructions of the visible cartons.

"Are those all from the one Italian firm?" I asked Greg, wishing he wouldn't grip my shoulder so hard.

He nodded. "Van Osten did more business than the size of his office would indicate. His territory covered five states."

"You've been to his office then."

"Early this morning. I'm glad you didn't leave any evidence of your . . . visit."

"What visit?" I smiled at him and removed his hand, massaging my shoulder where it hurt.

From the crate, Windfeldt called, "Nothing so far." He motioned for the stevedores to drop another side.

"I'd be interested to know if van Osten had branches of his smuggling network elsewhere," I said.

"Yes, I imagine Customs will be very interested, too." Greg's eyes did not leave the crate.

Another side crashed down, and Windfeldt disappeared around a corner.

I hated to stand by doing nothing. "Is there any reason we can't help him look?"

"Why not?" Greg motioned me forward.

I went around the opposite end of the crate from Windfeldt. The cartons, their shipping labels exposed, towered above me. I started reading, craning my neck upward: MRS. JOAN ALBRITTON, JOAN'S UNIQUE ANTIQUES. It was directly in front of me, in the second row from the top.

"I've found it!" I called.

Greg and Windfeldt turned around with identical expressions of annoyance. Clearly, each had wanted to make the discovery himself.

"What are you, a Geiger counter?" Greg demanded.

We retreated a few feet, and the stevedores removed the cartons. In less than a minute they had freed the right one and deposited it on the ground at our feet. We all looked down as if it might explode.

Greg said to Windfeldt, "Well, Inspector, it's all yours."

Surprisingly, the Customs man smiled. "That's okay, Lieutenant. It's your case."

"No." Greg reached for the knife Windfeldt was offering. "It's Ms. McCone's case." He extended the knife to me.

I hesitated, then reached for it, and our fingers touched on the handle. "Thank you," I said.

He shook his head. "Like I said, it's your case."

I knelt and cut the tape that sealed the edges of the carton, carefully so I wouldn't damage its contents. I tore the remaining tape, bent the top back, then pulled off several layers of packing material, dropping it on the ground.

The paintings, in their cheap gilt frames, lined up neatly inside. I removed the first few. A couple of days ago, I would not have known, but now, having held the Bellini in my hands, I could tell they were fakes. I flipped through the others without taking them out of the box. They were all flimsy, gaudy affairs; all, that is, but the one in the very center.

I pulled it out with trembling hands and held it up. Behind me, Greg drew his breath in sharply.

The three richly robed kings knelt on a stable floor, offering their costly gifts. Their expressions of awe and devotion were living, timeless evidence of the artist's faith.

156

Greg said, "It's another part of the Bellini triptych."

I glanced up at him. "Then they're bringing the whole thing in."

He nodded. "That's the right half of the altarpiece. I recognize it from the illustration in the magazine article."

"Then we may have still another shipment coming."

"You're right; we may." He turned to Windfeldt. "How would you like to give us an on-the-spot opinion, Inspector? I have what I assume to be the central panel in my car."

A look of grim pleasure crossed the Customs man's face. "I'd be glad to."

I gave him the painting, and we went back to Greg's car. It took the inspector only minutes to verify that the two paintings were part of the same larger work.

"This, of course, is a preliminary statement," he warned us. "I'll need to examine the work more closely and contact Italian authorities before I make it official."

"You'll get that opportunity, Inspector," Greg said. He thanked him, then turned to me and said, "That does it. I'm going to pick up Harmon."

I frowned.

"What's wrong?"

It was hard to pin down, but I couldn't see Harmon killing Joan Albritton for her property. It was another of his frequent deals on the side, and, as Hank had said, Harmon was used to them falling through. Harmon killing van Osten for the Bellini was even more difficult to visualize.

There was too great a disparity between the richness of the Bellini and Harmon's vulgar, mass-produced world: his Sunset District palace, his flashy suits, his cutesy little office bar. Even though he knew the dollar value of the Bellini, I didn't think Harmon would risk killing for it. Unlike van Osten, Joan Albritton, or for that matter Greg Marcus, Harmon had no instinctive grasp of the masterpiece's real worth.

Yet Greg Marcus was a professional who didn't jump blindly to conclusions. And I had no reasonable alternative to suggest. Picking up Harmon would shed light on the smuggling operation, if not on the murders.

I said, "I'm just tired. It's been a rough week."

"Shall I drop you at your place?"

"Please. And let me know how you make out with Harmon."

"You're entitled to a full report. I'll call you this evening no matter what happens."

On the way home, I leaned my head back against the seat, fighting depression. Not only was the case completely out of my hands now, but also I feared the truth of the murders had somehow eluded both Greg and me.

# Twenty-four

At home, I ate lunch, washed my hair, and sat out on the fire escape to dry it. The alley was quiet, since it was a school day. Warm sun played on my shoulders, and in the distance a transistor radio trilled carefree Latin tunes. I watched a woman hang laundry on the back porch across the way. She had a great many diapers and worked with tired, heavy motions. Seeing her reminded me I had forgotten to return my mother's phone call. I went inside and dialed San Diego.

As usual, the McCone household was in a state of minor crisis. I listened patiently as my mother explained how my older brother John had been arrested for his outstanding traffic tickets. On top of that, he had lost his housepainting job, and my father, in a rare show of rigidity left over from his days as a U.S. Navy Chief, had refused to let John's wife, Karen, and the three kids stay with them until the storm blew over. All was well now, my mother having exercised

159

her usual calming influence, and four extra people weren't really a strain, the kids being small.

"Still, it's very hard on your father and me," my mother concluded, "the way your brothers cannot get along with the police."

To cheer her I said, "Well, *I* get along with the police. I kissed a homicide lieutenant last night."

"Oh, Sharon," my mother sighed, "you're not mixed up in a murder, are you?"

"No, ma," I lied.

"Oh. Is he nice-looking?"

"Yes, ma."

"Are you going to see him again?"

I was sorry I'd mentioned it. "Probably."

"Well, just don't you go getting pregnant." Next to arrest, pregnancy was my mother's chief worry; it was my two younger sisters' specialty.

"Mother! Have I ever gotten pregnant?"

"No, but it wasn't for lack of trying."

Much as I loved my family, it was a conversation like this that made me glad I lived over five hundred miles away from them.

By four that afternoon, I was pacing around my apartment, deep in gloomy frustration. The conviction that I had missed a crucial fact about Joan's murder nagged me, along with mounting boredom. At four thirty I left a message for Greg with my answering service: I would be at the Salem Street shop restoring order; at least it was useful work. Before I left, I checked the .38 that was still in my bag. No sense in being careless.

Putting the shop back together proved too much for me, though. After several feeble attempts, I gave up and sat down on the settee next to Clothilde. I stared at the headless dummy through the growing dusk. All dressed up in red sequins with no place to go, she seemed to radiate sympathy for my own purposelessness.

160

"Damn it, Clothilde, I know the answer to my question is right here in the shop! Trouble is, I haven't figured out the question yet."

Clothilde had no comment for me.

"Harmon is probably guilty of arson and of blackmailing his way into a smuggling scheme, but he's not going to crack and confess these murders, because he didn't do them. I've overlooked the most important piece in the puzzle."

The shop echoed with silence.

"And Greg. Greg has been on the wrong track all along. First he focused on Charlie, and now he's just as single-minded about Harmon. I think he's deliberately ignored something, but I don't know what or why."

Clothilde seemed bored with my company.

I got up and wandered over to Bruno, patting his head. "I wonder what'll happen to you, Bruno, now that Joan isn't around to defend you."

The dog's glassy eyes watched me.

"There's a single thread running through everything that's happened this week, but I can't pick it out."

Again the silence, deepening around me.

I understood how Joan could have become slightly unbalanced, spending her days in this dark shop with its echoes of the past. No wonder she talked to Clothilde and Bruno and the little boy in a sailor suit, trying to coax life out of them. I went down the aisle to Edwin of the Iron Shoes, alone in his gloomy corner.

The mannequin, as always, stared at the wall.

"Poor Edwin," I said. "You don't have anything to look at any more. What a comedown after the Bellini. Did you know it was a masterpiece, or hasn't your critical eye developed that much yet?"

Edwin looked away disdainfully, preferring a blank wall to my conversation.

"Edwin, it's dumb to stare at an empty wall. Why don't you turn around?"

Silence.

"Sharon McCone, you *are* going insane!" I exclaimed loudly. To Edwin I added, "It's not your fault you're unfriendly. You couldn't turn around if you wanted to. After all, Charlie nailed you to the floor."

I smiled, remembering Joan's sales gimmick. How long had she been playing her artful, much-rehearsed role with Edwin? For over two years, since the fall before her grandson, Christopher, died.

With a pang of regret, I remembered Joan looking keenly at me and asking, "Are you an art lover by any chance?" And then she had taken the same flight of fancy with Cara Ingalls, a woman surely not given to make-believe. Joan's dream world had been captivating to even the least imaginative people, though. And knowing, as I did now, that she had been a crook still could not stunt my delight in the dead woman's fantasies.

Like the fantasy of Edwin as an art lover.

*A sales gimmick.*

The sales gimmick had been conceived two years ago, in the fall, at a time when Joan had needed a great deal more money than the shop could bring in.

*Are you an art lover by any chance?*

Ben Harmon had planned to set Joan up in a new shop, and presumably they would have smuggled in more and more artworks. Would Edwin have been nailed down facing a wall there, too?

*An art lover.*

The first time I'd seen Edwin, he was looking at a painting of shepherds in a field.

*A sales gimmick.*

I began to tremble.

"Edwin," I whispered. "Edwin, why didn't you tell me?"

What else goes with a Madonna, a child, and three wise men?

Shepherds. Shepherds in a field with their flock.

And what had Paula said about art collectors?

162

Some of them got their kicks from the solitary enjoyment of forbidden masterpieces.

I rushed down the aisle to the phone by the cash register. When I lifted the receiver, though, there was no dial tone. Of course, the phone had been disconnected. Flipping off the little light on the counter, I picked up my bag and started across the dark room toward the front door.

Halfway there I stopped, listening to approaching footsteps in the street. I barely had time to dive behind the counter when a key turned in the lock.

# Twenty-five

The front door shut, and footsteps crossed the shop directly to Edwin.

I slipped my hand into my bag and grasped my gun, as the footsteps came back and went into the workroom.

I took the gun out and crept forward on my hands and knees until I reached the wall and ran my left hand up to the light switch. As I stood up, I snapped it on.

In the dim light, Cara Ingalls crouched on the workroom floor, holding a torch on a stack of framed and unframed canvasses. She looked up in shock, her face taking on a cornered expression. She wore all black, even to a little hat that shaded her face, the perfect burglar's ensemble.

"You won't find the Bellini there, Cara." I held the gun on her. "Put the flashlight down and get up."

She remained on her knees, tightening her grip on the light until her knuckles went white.

"I don't know what you mean. I'm inspecting the property. I'm going to buy it, you know."

"The police have both panels of the altarpiece. They want the one you have, too."

"What altarpiece? I don't know what you're talking about." Her yellow eyes darted from side to side.

"The one you bought from van Osten and his Italian partner. Did you provide him contacts with other collectors? How much of a cut of the profits did you get?"

"You know so much, you tell me."

"Not as much as Ben Harmon got, I bet."

"Harmon!" She spat out the name. "What do you know about Harmon?"

"I know he was part of the smuggling operation. How did he catch on to it?"

"You know too goddamned much. The cheap bastard caught on because of Joan's ridiculous behavior with that mannequin, what's-his-name?"

"Edwin."

"Edwin." She snorted. "Joan had to use a melodramatic way of identifying the collectors when they came in for their paintings. Harmon saw Joan was hipped on Edwin but only at certain times."

"And each of those times, someone bought a painting on Edwin's wall."

Ingalls laughed bitterly. "Joan was a whimsical fool. Oliver felt it a small price to keep her happy, but he never should have permitted it. When Harmon got curious, he wormed the rest out of the old bitch."

"And then?"

"Then he went to Oliver and put the squeeze on him. He wanted a cut, plus to expand the business with Joan in a bigger shop."

"And while he was at it, he also wanted her land."

Ingalls nodded. "And now I suppose *you* want something. How much will *you* cost me?"

I shook my head. "Like I said, the police have all of the

166

altarpiece except the shepherd panel you picked up here last fall. I want to know how the smuggling operation fell apart."

Her eyes glittered. "I can't tell you anything about that."

"Not about murdering Joan Albritton? And Oliver van Osten?"

Her face went pale; then her hand moved quickly and she hurled the flashlight at my head. As I ducked, Ingalls sprang at me, knocking me to the floor. My gun flew from my hand.

I pulled myself up against the wall, looking for the gun, but before I could find it, Ingalls was on me, a daggerlike knife in her hand. It was the one missing from the bone-handled set.

I froze with fear, my eyes on the sharp, double-edged blade as she brought it closer to my throat. I remembered the blood soaking into van Osten's pale-yellow carpet. Cara Ingalls knew how to use this knife very, very well.

"You want to know about Albritton and van Osten, do you?" Her eyes were inches from mine, and the knife tip touched the hollow of my throat.

I forced down terror, knowing it would incite her. The lack of control that I had sensed the day before showed in her eyes now. Keeping my voice as level as I could, I said, "You didn't really intend to kill Joan, did you?"

Cara Ingalls's breath touched my face in hot little gasps as her amber eyes searched mine. Then, surprisingly, she dropped back a couple of inches, not off her guard but no longer touching me. The pressure of the knife decreased.

"I didn't intend to kill anyone." She was trembling. "Van Osten had raised the price on the remainder of the altarpiece. He knew the shepherd panel was no use to me without the others."

"That wasn't fair. Why did he do it?" I was leaning against the wall, my left leg curled under me, but it hurt too much to give me leverage. Ingalls crouched in front of me, her knife a deterrent to any movement. I couldn't see my gun in the dim light.

"He knew I killed Albritton. He came in and found me

with the body." Her husky voice became shrill. My question had struck at Ingalls's need for emotional attention, the same need she'd displayed the day before when she told me the story of her father canceling his life insurance. Probably, in her climb to the top, she'd taken no one as a confidante. As she had begun to break down under the pressure of murder and blackmail, I had appeared, a woman who, however briefly, would listen to her.

I encouraged her need. "What happened with Albritton?"

She shuddered. "I came here to the shop on Monday night to persuade her to sell the remaining Bellinis and the land directly to me. Van Osten, acting for Harmon, had threatened to hold out on the last two panels unless I withdrew my bid for the land. Also, the smuggling operation was falling apart. Our Italian contact was having trouble getting the stolen paintings into the factory shipments. There was a four-month delay between the first and second panels for my altarpiece, for instance. I knew it was time to act. But then that stupid bitch told me she was pulling out of the scheme and didn't owe me a thing. We argued, and she said a terrible thing to me. I saw the knives in the open cabinet and . . ."

Her voice faltered, and she almost lowered the knife. I began to straighten, and the blade came back up.

Quickly I asked, "What was it she said?"

A spasm, more violent than before, shook her. "She called me a vulture. She said I spent my life feasting off the remains of people I'd destroyed. She said I wasn't human, that I was a sick, disgusting thing to her."

I shivered, remembering Joan's last words to Charlie Cornish: "You're nothing to me now." Her revulsion at Ingalls was probably an extension of her own self-hatred because of her cruelty to Charlie.

Watching me so closely, Ingalls softened. "Isn't that the most awful thing to say to a person?"

I nodded. It was awful, but not bad enough to kill for. In

vain, I looked around for my gun. "And then van Osten walked in?"

"Yes. He'd come to collect the Madonna so I wouldn't be able to get my hands on it until he'd forced me to withdraw my bid. He told me to get out of here and let him take care of things. It wasn't until I got to my car that I realized I still had the knife in my hand. It was all covered with blood and sticky." She made a disgusted face.

How unpleasant for you, I thought. Aloud I asked, "When did you hear from van Osten again?"

"The next day. He called me and raised the price of the Madonna."

"And you went to his apartment last night to pay him?" My left leg didn't hurt so much now, and I started to brace it against the wall. Ingalls was talking swiftly, uncontrollably. If I knew where my gun was, I could take her off guard.

"But he didn't have the painting. He told me to forget it, said he'd even resorted to Ben Harmon's arson tactics to get hold of it, but it was no use. Instead, he had this plan that we should ditch Harmon, that I should buy the land after all, and go in with him on a really big smuggling operation. With my contacts with collectors, he said we'd have it made. I knew what that meant; I'd be under his thumb for the rest of my life. I had to protect myself. I had to cover up . . ."

"So you used a knife."

Her pupils were dilated, her eyes straining. "I didn't mean to kill him!" She blinked hard for an instant.

But I had seen van Osten lying on the blood-soaked yellow carpet. And right now I also saw my gun, lying near the baseboard to the left. I braced my heel against the wall. Reflexively, Ingalls brought the knife up again.

"No way, Cara," I said, cruelly. "No way."

She looked shocked at my withdrawal of sympathy. "What do you mean, 'no way'?"

"People who don't plan to kill don't take knives to their business meetings, especially knives they've killed with be-

169

fore." As I said it, I pushed into her, knocking her backwards and grabbing at the knife. It sliced across the palm of my hand and blood spurted. Crying in pain, I fell on top of her and smashed the knife from her grip. It clattered to the floor.

I forced her down and reached toward my gun. I couldn't get to it and keep her down at the same time. She began to fight back and struggle for the knife. As we fought, the front door of the shop opened.

Greg Marcus's voice called, "Sharon? Cara? Where are you?"

Ingalls threw me off and bolted toward the front room. I jumped up and went after her, screaming, "Stop her! She's the murderer!"

As I chased Ingalls through the room I saw Greg by the door, his gun drawn. Why in hell didn't he shoot?

I hurled myself at Ingalls, pulled her down, pinned her arm behind her back. She gave a cry that ended in a grunt and lay still. From the limpness of her body, I knew the fall had stunned her.

Panting, I looked up at Greg, who stood frozen.

"Do something, damn it!" I cried. "She killed both of them over the Bellini! She was part of the whole scheme!"

He gestured to a uniformed man who had come in behind him, then lowered his gun and stepped forward, reaching out a hand to help me up. He looked deeply shocked. "Are you all right?"

I looked down at our clasped hands. They were smeared with blood. I pulled mine away and brushed my hair back. More blood came off on my face.

Greg snatched my hand from my hair and spread my fingers, palm up. He said in relief, "It's only a small cut. It's deep, but you'll live. Otherwise, are you okay?"

Anger rose up, replacing my fear. "Yes, I'll live, no thanks to you! Why didn't you stop her?"

He shook his head and pulled me against him. After a few seconds he said, "Jesus, I'm sorry, Sharon! When I got the message you left with your answering service, I decided to put a man back on the shop. We hadn't been able to pick up Frankie, and I didn't want you here alone. Cara's company car was outside. I thought it had something to do with the sale of the property . . ."

He broke off, and we hung on to one another for a minute. Then he released me, looking down at the prone figure of Cara Ingalls. She hadn't moved. He said, "Get up, Cara."

She raised her head, her face dull with shock. "Don't, Greg."

I glanced from one to the other in confusion. "You know her?"

Greg nodded, his lips twisting. "This is the woman friend I told you about. The one who opened my eyes to the world of art."

I caught my breath sharply and looked at him, not speaking. It explained a great many things.

Greg looked back at Ingalls, who was up on one elbow now. "I said get up, Cara."

Cara Ingalls brought herself to a sitting position, but then her strength seemed to fail her. Her hair had fallen over one eye, and she had lost her little black hat. She pushed the hair back, then fixed her eyes on Marcus.

"Don't, Greg." She stretched out a hand to him.

Greg left her on the floor. In an empty, impersonal voice he began, "You have the right to remain silent. You have the right . . ."

Cara Ingalls's face contorted as if she might suddenly begin screaming, and if she did, her screams would never stop.

171

# Twenty-six

Hank Zahn, Charlie Cornish, and I sat around the table by
the big kitchen window at All Souls. Below us, the city slept,
a few pre-dawn lights winking. It was five in the morning,
and we'd consumed most of a gallon of cheap California
mountain red.

I'd seen a doctor about my hand, made my official
statement, and gone directly to the law cooperative to report
to Hank. There, I remembered my promise to Charlie and
called the big junkman to tell him I'd found Joan's killer. He
insisted on coming to All Souls to hear my story in person.

Now Charlie said, "If I'd known that bitch murdered
Joanie when she came to get the key tonight, I'd have killed
her with my bare hands."

Hank and I nodded in drunken agreement.

"Jesus, she comes to me, demanding that key like she
already owned the place. Big realtor car outside. Says she

173

wants to inspect the property. Acted like I was dirt. Looked around my shop like germs might come out of the corners and bite her ass. I wish I'd killed her!"

"I'm just as glad you didn't," Hank said, "because I'd be down at the city jail defending you rather than here at home drinking wine. Besides, then the whole story never would have come out."

Charlie grunted. "Don't count on that. By now the bitch has some hotshot lawyer there, making sure she doesn't say anything."

I shook my head. "Ingalls waived her right to counsel and made a full confession to Greg Marcus, her great lover. I'm surprised he would let her confess: he was blind to her from the start. Even when he saw me chasing her around the shop, he just stood there. . . ." My voice broke. I felt Greg had let me down, first at the shop and next by turning coldly professional on me at police headquarters. I had needed support, injured and shocked as I was, but he had offered none.

Hank glanced at me anxiously. "Don't be too hard on him, Sharon. It's not every day he has to arrest his former mistress for murder. And you have to think of how he feels now—pretty much like an asshole after standing by and watching you do his work for him."

I looked down at my bandaged hand. The doctor had said there would be a scar—a souvenir I really didn't want. "He probably hates me, too, for opening the whole thing up. I think he suspected Cara's involvement from the beginning but pushed it to the back of his mind."

"That would be natural," Hank said, "even for a cop as good as Greg. You remember I said Greg had been the cause of a society divorce? It was Cara and Douglas Ingalls who split up."

I felt a flash of jealousy at Hank's words, then a flash of annoyance at my jealousy. "So why didn't he marry her and keep her out of trouble?"

Hank smiled. "She was willing, but Greg found he couldn't

handle the idea of a wife who made more money than he did. It was hard for him to accept that Cara didn't need him in any of the traditional ways women need men.

"Besides," he added, "her plans for Greg were kind of bizarre, if you know Greg like I do."

"What plans?" I heard the open hostility in my voice.

Hank must have heard it, too, because he chuckled. "Mrs. Ingalls couldn't be married to a cop—it would never do in her social circle. Greg was to quit the force and devote himself to the finer things in life, like servicing Cara and broadening his interest in the arts when she was busy elsewhere. She even offered to pay for painting lessons."

I smiled, reluctantly. Hank's words conjured up a picture of Greg in a smock, seated at an easel, palette in hand, looking faintly ridiculous. "So he turned her down?"

Hank nodded. "Greg's a cop through and through. It hurt that she professed to love him yet hadn't grasped the single most important fact of his existence. He turned her down, and she threatened suicide. Since he'd seen through her by then, he told her he wasn't worried, she was too self-centered to do anything foolish. Cara threw a lamp, two vases, and an ashtray at him, left, and carried on her life in style."

I asked, "So it's been over for a long time?"

"For more than three years. I think the first time Greg saw her since they finished must have been when you flattened her on the floor of the shop." Hank paused, sipping thoughtfully at his wine.

"You know," he went on, "Greg's initial reaction to you was colored by his experience with Cara. He sensed the same strength and independence in you, so he set out to put you in your place. Fortunately, you wouldn't stay put."

I grimaced. "He tried damned hard though."

Hank laughed. "You don't know how frustrated it made him! By Wednesday night, he'd recognized the futility of his efforts and called me, babbling with hostility and demanding I order you back to All Souls, where you belonged. I pointed out what an ass he was making of himself and how it linked to his bad time with Cara. I also advised him that strength in a woman didn't necessarily indicate ruthlessness or indifference to others. When we got done yelling at each other, he seemed much calmer.''

Wednesday night. So that was the "talking to" Greg had mentioned to me at the museum, the one he'd told me to ask Hank about.

"Well, I thank you." I raised my glass to Hank. "Your lecture turned him into quite a likable human being. It's too bad he's not going to want to see me again after that scene in the antique shop."

Hank raised an eyebrow. "Were you planning to see him again?"

"Oh, sure. He was going to teach me all about Cézanne."

Hank frowned. "I thought you couldn't stand him. Greg, I mean, not Cézanne." The words were teasing.

With dignity I said, "We're all entitled to change our minds."

Hank looked across the table at Charlie. "I'll never understand women."

"Huh?" Charlie jerked up. He'd been dozing over his wine.

"Women. I don't understand them."

"Yeah? Well, don't look at me," Charlie said. "I've never understood 'em either. Joanie used to tell me I was an old fool where she was concerned, and I guess she was right. But, damn it, I *liked* being a fool for her."

Hank's eyes sobered. "She was one hell of a fine woman. We'll all miss her."

"God, yes. Every day I wake up, expecting to see her; then I realize there's something wrong, and it all comes back to me." He drew at his wine, looking melancholy. "Somehow, now that they've got her killer, I feel a little more at peace. And making a clean breast of what happened between her and me that night, that helps some, too. I think soon I can get on to remembering the good times."

176

Hank and I nodded. Hank looked drunkenly solemn, and I was sure my expression matched his.

"You think Sharon should see the lieutenant again, Charlie?" Hank had a mischievous gleam in his eyes.

Charlie looked at me speculatively. "Sure. He's a good-looking man, and she's wasting her better years hanging around with guys like you and me."

Quietly I said, "You forget that in all likelihood the lieutenant does not want to see me."

"Nonsense," Hank said. "He wants to see you."

I caught my breath. "How do you know?"

Hank grinned broadly. "He called me while you were on the phone with Charlie before. Said I should use my judgment, but if you weren't too bitter against him, would I ask you to call him. He'll be in his office around eight."

"Hank Zahn, why didn't you tell me before?"

"I repeat, he said to use my judgment. And you sounded bitter as hell when you first told me what had happened."

"Oh." I looked down into the depths of my wine glass. "Oh, no, I'm not bitter." I realized that Greg had hidden in his professional disguise at police headquarters out of embarrassment at my part in Cara's arrest. Quickly I changed the subject. "So what happens now, Charlie? Who will you sell the property to?"

He grinned. "Seeing as our two highest bidders are in jail, I guess I'll have to throw it open to new offers. I'm not worried; there'll be plenty."

"You still moving to Valencia Street?" Hank asked. "Or won't you take the place now that Bigby's lost all his stock in the fire?"

"No reason not to," Charlie said. "Austin doesn't have much stuff, but he's got a lot of expertise to bring to the new shop. Besides, I've got more merchandise and capital than I need for myself, what with Joanie leaving me everything."

I didn't say it, but I thought of where a lot of that capital had come from.

177

"Aw, Sharon, I know what you're thinking," Charlie said. "Ill-gotten gains. Well, forget it. What Joanie did was illegal, but she did it for the kid, not herself. Everything Joanie ever did was for other people, not herself."

"I'll forget it." I was relieved that Charlie wasn't going to let anything tarnish his feelings for Joan.

"The stock from Joanie's shop will replace what Austin lost," Charlie went on, "but that brings up this problem I've got."

Hank and I looked at him questioningly.

"Edwin and Clothilde I'm happy to move to the new shop," he said. "I could never give either of them up. But the hell of it is, I feel honor-bound to move that goddamn stuffed dog, too!"

I smiled, and Hank got up to pour more wine from the big jug. We sat drinking in companionable silence, watching the morning sun light up the glass towers of downtown San Francisco.

After a while, I glanced at my watch. It was six o'clock. In two hours I'd call Greg at his office to suggest we get together and talk things over.